M000169552

DEAL WITH
THE DEVIL

SEAL Brotherhood: Legacy Series
Book 4

SHARON HAMILTON

SHARON HAMILTON'S BOOK LIST

SEAL BROTHERHOOD BOOKS

SEAL BROTHERHOOD SERIES
Accidental SEAL Book 1
Fallen SEAL Legacy Book 2
SEAL Under Covers Book 3
SEAL The Deal Book 4
Cruisin' For A SEAL Book 5
SEAL My Destiny Book 6
SEAL of My Heart Book 7
Fredo's Dream Book 8
SEAL My Love Book 9
SEAL Encounter Prequel to Book 1
SEAL Endeavor Prequel to Book 2
Ultimate SEAL Collection Vol. 1 Books 1-4 /2 Prequels
Ultimate SEAL Collection Vol. 2 Books 5-7

SEAL BROTHERHOOD LEGACY SERIES
Watery Grave Book 1
Honor The Fallen Book 2
Grave Injustice Book 3
Deal With The Devil Book 4

BAD BOYS OF SEAL TEAM 3 SERIES
SEAL's Promise Book 1
SEAL My Home Book 2
SEAL's Code Book 3
Big Bad Boys Bundle Books 1-3

BAND OF BACHELORS SERIES

Lucas Book 1

Alex Book 2

Jake Book 3

Jake 2 Book 4

Big Band of Bachelors Bundle

BONE FROG BROTHERHOOD SERIES

New Year's SEAL Dream Book 1

SEALed At The Altar Book 2

SEALed Forever Book 3

SEAL's Rescue Book 4

SEALed Protection Book 5

Bone Frog Brotherhood Superbundle

BONE FROG BACHELOR SERIES

Bone Frog Bachelor Book 0.5

Unleashed Book 1

Restored Book 2

Revenge Book 3

SUNSET SEALS SERIES

SEALed at Sunset Book 1

Second Chance SEAL Book 2

Treasure Island SEAL Book 3

Escape to Sunset Book 4

The House at Sunset Beach Book 5

Second Chance Reunion Book 6

Love's Treasure Book 7

Finding Home Book 8 (releasing summer 2022)

Sunset SEALs Duet #1

Sunset SEALs Duet #2

LOVE VIXEN

Bone Frog Love

SHADOW SEALS

Shadow of the Heart

Shadow Warrior

SILVER SEALS SERIES

SEAL Love's Legacy

SLEEPER SEALS SERIES

Bachelor SEAL

STAND ALONE BOOKS & SERIES

SEAL's Goal: The Beautiful Game

Nashville SEAL: Jameson

True Blue SEALS Zak

Paradise: In Search of Love

Love Me Tender, Love You Hard

NOVELLAS

SEAL You In My Dreams Magnolias and Moonshine

PARANORMALS

GOLDEN VAMPIRES OF TUSCANY SERIES
Honeymoon Bite Book 1
Mortal Bite Book 2
Christmas Bite Book 3
Midnight Bite Book 4

THE GUARDIANS
Heavenly Lover Book 1
Underworld Lover Book 2
Underworld Queen Book 3
Redemption Book 4

FALL FROM GRACE SERIES
Gideon: Heavenly Fall

NOVELLAS
SEAL Of Time Trident Legacy

All of Sharon's books are available on Audible, narrated by the talented J.D. Hart.

Copyright © 2022 by Sharon Hamilton
Print Edition

All rights reserved. Without limiting the rights under copyright reserved above, no part of this publication may be reproduced, stored in or introduced into a retrieval system, or transmitted, in any form, or by any means (electronic, mechanical, photocopying, recording, or otherwise) without the prior written permission of the copyright owner of this book.

This is a work of fiction. Names, characters, places, brands, media, and incidents are either the product of the author's imagination or are used fictitiously. In many cases, liberties and intentional inaccuracies have been taken with rank, description of duties, locations and aspects of the SEAL community.

ABOUT THE BOOK

An enemy from the past threatens Nick and Devon's winery and lavender farm.

Set in the lush, bucolic landscape of Sonoma County's Wine Country, former Navy SEAL Nick Dunn finds life and love after his time on the Teams.

But danger lurks around every corner, and Nick will do whatever it takes to protect his loved ones

You don't want to miss this steamy SEAL romance! More details coming soon…

AUTHOR'S NOTE

I always dedicate my SEAL Brotherhood books to the brave men and women who defend our shores and keep us safe. Without their sacrifice, and that of their families—because a warrior's fight always includes his or her family—I wouldn't have the freedom and opportunity to make a living writing these stories. They sometimes pay the ultimate price so we can debate, argue, go have coffee with friends, raise our children and see them have children of their own.

One of my favorite tributes to warriors resides on many memorials, including one I saw honoring the fallen of WWII on an island in the Pacific:

"When you go home
Tell them of us, and say
For your tomorrow,
We gave our today."

These are my stories created out of my own imagination. Anything that is inaccurately portrayed is either my mistake, or done intentionally to disguise something I might have overheard over a beer or in the corner of one of the hangouts along the Coronado Strand.

I support two main charities. Navy SEAL/UDT Museum operates in Ft. Pierce, Florida. Please learn about this wonderful museum, all run by active and former SEALs and their friends and families, and who rely on public support, not that of the U.S. Government. www.navysealmuseum.org

IF YOU GOT ANY CLOSER, YOU WOULD HAVE TO ENLIST

I also support Wounded Warriors, who tirelessly bring together the warrior as well as the family members who are just learning to deal with their soldier's condition and have nowhere to turn. It is a long path to becoming well, but I've seen first-hand what this organization does for its warriors and the families who love them. Please give what your heart tells you is right. If you cannot give, volunteer at one of the many service centers all over the United States. Get involved. Do something meaningful for someone who gave so much of themselves, to families who have paid the price for your freedom. You'll find a family there unlike any other on the planet.

www.woundedwarriorproject.org

CHAPTER 1

ORMER NAVY SEAL Nicholas Dunn watched his wife and two daughters throwing a flour storm in his kitchen. It was one of the most messy, happy, and frivolous sights he'd witnessed in a long time. His two daughters, Laurel, seven years old, and Lilly Dunn, eight years old, were learning to help their mother prepare pies and treats for guests at their wedding center and winery/lavender farm, Sophie's Choice. It had been nearly nine years since he and Devon took over the formerly battered and bruised nursery property left to them by Nick's sister, Sophie.

Now they had a world-class destination center for weddings, an award-winning merlot vineyard said to be one of the best in Sonoma County, and a top-rated lavender farm. It had started out to be a cottage industry for them but soon progressed into a full-scale operation—but the girls and Devon still got their hands working, making the wonderful-smelling products that helped create their lifestyle.

Sophie had dreamed one day to have something like what Nick, Devon, and their girls had. He remembered that every day. And was grateful.

In three days, after several other events already on the books, they were to be hosting a wedding for one of his former teammates on SEAL Team 3, Joshua, and his bride-to-be, Amanda.

But today, all of the hard work for setting up the reception area was off in the distance, and they were focusing on creating luscious treats for a luncheon the next day.

This morning, he'd already finished a round of light tractor work in the lavender fields and had plowed under the fields for the vineyard, although most of the heavy work and routine maintenance of the property was left to his grounds crew and vineyard management team. Nick had a hard time not getting his boots dirty and working the land, though, to commune with the spirit of his deceased sister, fulfilling the dream she'd had, even talking to her every day while he was doing it. He gave her updates.

"Sophie, you'd love how the lavender is coming along. Got some special golden lavender, which was originally grown in the Red Sea region during the time of Christ. It smells just like the purple variety from France, but perhaps with hints of lemon and grapefruit."

In the morning sun, he had continued with his up-dates, as if she was the CEO managing things from Heaven.

"Funny how all the wine critics use those scents in their notes about the Merlot. It's the first time I've ever read that. But they do, as if somehow the lavender feeds the grapes and perhaps vice-versa."

He'd walked down one row, discovered a broken water line, and stopped to repair it, making a note on the little pad of paper he carried constantly with his cell phone in his breast pocket.

"Gotta tell the guys to watch for these. When the crews aren't careful, they are easy to break. We can't afford to waste any water," he'd mumbled as he jotted down the notes.

While their hard work had developed the property into the world-class vineyard that his sister had always wanted to have, Nick felt he and Devon had walked into the life Sophie really deserved. The worst part for him was experiencing the joy of his family without her there to laugh and encourage them on.

So he created this imaginary dialogue with her, and somehow, that made him feel better about it. He liked the idea that he could tell his story to his sister, and he knew how much she'd love hearing it, even if she could watch it out unfold real-time from above.

As the years went by, he'd gotten better at removing those storm clouds from his head and refused to remember those dark times—Sophie's last days there at dilapidated nursery. Now, watching the most important women in his life tossing fistfuls of flour at each other, getting it in their hair, down their backs, and sometimes landing a toss square in each other's mouths, he was again filled with gratitude and pride. He'd have to say everything in his life was now perfect.

Their littlest daughter, Sophia, was taking a nap.

When he was on SEAL Team 3, serving under his LPO Kyle Lansdowne and with all the other men that he had at one time sworn he'd died to protect, he'd never thought he'd enjoy being an event planner of the "ultimate Wine Country experience," living in the heart of Sonoma County's world-class foodie Mecca to bring in tourists, or farming a vineyard hangout that attracted travelers from all over the world. He'd never seen himself tending to little lavender plants that would bloom and make oils, elixirs, even aperitifs. He hadn't imagined stomping grapes and bottling the fermented juice of the Gods or catering to families who wanted to stage a lavish Sonoma County destination wedding event to rival all others. It just wasn't part of who he was at the time.

Devon had originally thought him to be so cocky and full of himself, and Nicholas figured yeah, he probably had been. But the love of his wife and the time caring for this little piece of heaven taught him that his higher calling and his real purpose was to raise his family and his girls, be a farmer, and change the energy of the whole world by doing luscious and creative, tasteful things rather than raiding villages and trying to catch bad guys.

This part of his life—and he never forgot to thank Sophie (and ask her to tell God, because Nick didn't pray)—was filled with peace and love. Had he earned this? Or was it just luck?

Not that he didn't want to rid the world of bad guys. It just wasn't his job now.

When the neighbor put arsenic in Sophie's water tank, effectively killing her, he had to go after that particular bad guy. But now, with the murderer safely tucked away in prison, likely never to be released on parole, Nick's life was simpler. The winery next door, still owned by the Rodriguez family, had been allowed to go into disrepair, the lack of water causing the vineyard to shrivel up and die. The only thing keeping it alive before the owner went to prison was the fact that he was stealing water from Sophie's well by lateral drilling on land near the property boundary. After the discovery of the arsenic, they had tested the water and were reassured that only the water tank was contaminated, not the source of the well.

The girls were having such a great time he didn't want to interrupt. He left the kitchen area and wandered out into the pavilion, the big open-air room where they had receptions, parties, weddings, and everything in between. They even hosted several SEAL Team 3 reunion parties that were a pure joy to put on.

He studied the tall rafters, glass skylights, and stained-glass windows overlapping the clerestory openings. Beautiful silk and patchwork curtains hung down when they raised the rollup doors and allowed the air to freely blow through, bringing with it the scent of lavender and, in the Fall, the scent of fermenting grapes that had fallen to the ground. It was something magical about this area.

The beauty of it, the entrance to the valley of the moon, that legendary place where Jack London wrote, was always breathtaking. And on full moons, that silver orb rested in the dark sky with a smattering of stars everywhere, shining down the valley floor and illuminating the tree lines on both sides of the valley. It was special. It was about as untouched as any civilized part of wine country could be. It wasn't overrun with tourists, although they had a steady stream of visitors year-round.

Nick and Devon raised their money mostly by operating the wedding center, where they also custom-bottled vintages for weddings and special occasions, as well as made special products out of the lavender oils for the guests. The lavender products enhanced the winery's visitor center as that in turn enhanced the wedding center, in a symbiotic relationship Nick was proud of.

They were going to build a four-cottage guest chalet on the corner of the property where they could host short-term weekend guests or week-long stays through several worldwide sites. He and Devon had envisioned this ecotourism business, people coming up from San Francisco, the Peninsula, or the Bay Area to spend a weekend or a week learning how to cultivate grapes, an organic vegetable garden, and products from lavender. He had eight different varieties of lavender, varying from Spanish to French to other exotic forms of lavender that even grew in the Baltic and several other regions of the world. Some of them very rare.

He inhaled as he looked up to the ceiling and let the sunshine wash over him. It was so perfect he hardly could believe how lucky he was.

Walking back into the house, the first thing he heard was Sophia's little voice coming from the back bedroom.

Devon called out to him.

"Can you get her? I'm a little tied up," she said, holding her hands up. She was covered with flour from her fingertips to her elbows, also extending to parts of her cheek, her nose, and into her hair. The girls both looked up at him inquisitively.

"No problem." He ran down the hallway toward Sophie's room. "I'm coming, Soph. Daddy's right here."

"Daddy! I had a bad dream," Sophie mumbled as he entered her room and turned on the Pooh Bear table lamp.

Nick sat on the edge of her bed. He'd made his opinion known that he thought she was placed in her own room a little too soon. And Devon had taken away her crib, replacing it with a single bed.

"What's going on, Sophie?"

"I think there are monsters underneath my bed."

That's when Nick knew that his assessment been correct. They should have moved her into the room in her crib first and then taken the crib away and given her own bed. But they didn't do that. They did it all at once, and she had been waking up at night all week since they'd separated her from her older sisters.

"Now you know that Daddy would take care of any kind of monsters if they were underneath your bed. And I don't hear them or see them. Maybe you only see them in your dreams?"

"Yes. I see them in my dreams. And you can't go into my dreams, Daddy, or can you?"

Nick was glad she thought he was capable of doing

such a thing but chuckled nonetheless. He tussled the top of her hair, held her up close to him, and gave her a hug.

"Sophie, there are lots of things at night, and in our dreams, that scare us. Even us grownups have nightmares sometimes. But just remember, you can always come in to see Mommy and Daddy. You can always come into our bed, no problem. And if you ask for me in the middle of the night, I'll be sure to come. So you're very safe. No monster is going to last once I get in here. You know that, right?"

"Yes, Daddy." She folded her hands together when Nicholas released her and brushed her own hair out of her face, very much like a teenager, like Laurel and Lilly were fast approaching.

"I haven't wet the bed, though, and I'm happy about that. Maybe I'm just afraid to wet the bed. Maybe that's why I keep waking up. But I hear sounds, and I hear the animals outside."

Nick looked at her window, which was ajar, and he thought about that for a second and then walked over and closed it. "There. I think it's a better idea if we keep this window closed. Don't you?"

"Definitely."

One thing his daughter had inherited from her namesake—Nicholas's sister, Sophie—was her stubbornness and her ability to verbalize her needs in succinct commands. It was amazing how much the two of them were alike. Sophie would've enjoyed playing with her niece.

"I think that'll make it better. So let's try that for a while. And if you want, you can have one of your sisters come in here and sleep with you. Or we could move a roll-up bed in here, and they could both sleep with you for a few nights if you like that."

"No, Daddy. They will tease me. They'll call me a baby. I'm a big girl. I don't want them to do that."

"I get you, Sweetheart. Don't worry about that. They love you, and they just want you to be able to sleep and not to be afraid. And if they tease you, well, you just let us know, and we'll take care of it."

"Daddy, I have to go pee."

Nicholas stood up and watched as Sophia passed by him, went into the Jack and Jill bathroom between Lilly and Laurel's room and Sophie's, and closed the door, but before she did so, she snuck a peek back at her Daddy to make sure he wasn't going to follow.

Nicholas brought Sophia into the kitchen, balancing her on his hip while he made coffee with one hand and poured a cup of juice for her. The girls had started sweeping and cleaning up the floor, and Devon had cleaned up the countertop after all the pastry dough had been rolled out. She'd placed them into pans, fluted the dough, added the berry mixture and the tops, and completed all the decorations on the pies and the tarts, and they were set on the stovetop while the oven heated.

"Those look fantastic. Looks like we're going to feed a hundred here," Nick said. He counted six mixed berry pies and a dozen tartlets.

"Well, you know how it is when the berries come in. You have to use them up. I did add a few strawberries, though, because I was slightly short. I think they're going to be delicious."

Devon wiped a lock of hair away from her forehead. She had not cleaned her face, so the flour on her nose and both cheeks gave away the fact she was not a high-powered realtor anymore. She was a homemaker, a businesswoman, a woman entrepreneur, and Nick's amazing partner and wife. Her jams and jellies and pies were legendary in the county. Although she still dabbled a little bit in real estate, he liked her looking this way, with her hair disheveled, her face covered in flour, and surrounded by the other two important ladies of his life.

"I have to say, Devon—" he admitted as he looked at her with a smile, "—you get more and more beautiful as the years go by. I can't believe it's been ten years since we got together. It's just gone by so fast."

She blushed, even through her floured cheeks. "Well, it was not the life I expected to live, but it turned out to be the one that I love. I wish Sophie were here, though. I really do. But I'm happy that we carry on her legacy."

Lilly looked up at her mom. "Was Aunt Sophie... Did she look like my sister, or did she look more like Daddy?"

Devon chuckled and then thought about the question for a moment before answering.

"I think she looked a lot like little Sophia. Nicholas is kind of... I just don't see Sophie too much in him, even though they were brother and sister. But Sophia looks a lot like her," said Devon.

"How old was Aunt Sophie when she died?"

"She was, I believe, forty-one. Maybe forty-two?" Devon looked at Nicholas.

"Forty-one. Way too young."

THE GROUP GATHERING the next day was a women's business conference, taking up the pavilion, with a luncheon and a trade show for women entrepreneurs. Nicholas and Devon had agreed to lease the property almost at cost for startup companies and minority and women-run businesses. The goodwill it generated for their winery business and their lavender mail order business grew, nearly doubling every year for the past four years. This group of ladies was well dressed, sipping coffee and sampling Devon's fruit tarts as they mingled after the luncheon was over. They'd had a motivational speaker talking about success and making lemonade out of lemons, someone who had survived years as a trafficked teenager and had grown into a very powerful and successful businesswoman. It was an inspiring speech.

Doris Calhoun, who was also one of their neighbors, approached him.

"You know, I've seen some activity over at the winery there." She pointed over her shoulder like tossing salt over her back. "Have you noticed it?"

Nicholas honestly hadn't and shook his head. "No."

"I've seen them clearing out some vines and planting fruit trees of all things. Don't they need water? Who would do such a thing?"

"What kind of trees?" Nick asked.

"They look like apples or pears. Do you know anything about it? Has it sold, because I haven't heard anything?" Mrs. Calhoun asked.

"That's completely news to me, and I haven't heard or seen anybody working over there. I thought they were just leaving it fallow."

Mrs. Calhoun continued, "The family, from last I heard, was fighting over who was going to take over, but nobody knew how to run a winery, and with no water, that's a huge problem."

"You're right. I'm not about to deal with those

people, so they aren't going to get water from us."

"I should hope not. We'd all be up in arms if you offered."

It was disturbing for Nicholas, though, to hear the news about somebody working on the property, and he decided perhaps he'd asked Devon to check the tax records and go in to see if there was some kind of a change in ownership or the tax. They needed to find out who had paid the taxes and fees that would still be ongoing even though they weren't running the winery. Property taxes in California still would continue, and it would be based on the potential of the grapes, even though, one by one, they were all dying and were going to need replacement before the vineyard property could be honestly worked.

But it was a small gray cloud in the distant horizon for Nicholas. Nothing he couldn't research and arm himself with information against, just in case.

He reassured her. "I'll check it out. Don't worry. I don't think anybody's done anything. And he's in forever. I mean, we have to be notified if he ever gets out, and I've not received any information about any kind of a parole hearing or a new petition. So I'd say the odds are pretty bad that anything's going to happen."

"That's good. I'm sure glad you and Devon are our neighbors here. I don't ever want you guys to leave.

Don't you go back to San Diego where all your buddies are, Nick. I know that still holds some attraction for you, but we need you here in Sonoma County. And I like the fact that my next-door neighbor is a crack shot."

Nicholas laughed at that. "I'm not so sure how good a shot I am. I haven't been practicing regularly, but I've gone on a couple trips with some of my buddies."

She raised her eyebrows.

"Not to worry that it's a secret need-to-know basis. They were hunting trips. All legal."

Satisfied, Mrs. Calhoun waved at him and wandered off to talk to several of her other ladies.

The next big event being held was the wedding for Joshua and Amanda in two days, but people would begin arriving in one. Nicholas had very briefly known the groom-to-be when he was active on Seal Team 3, but they had become friends later because Joshua's parents lived in Santa Rosa. He frequently visited with them and always stopped by to say hello to Nick and Devon. Joshua kept asking them if someday, when he got out of the teams, they might consider taking him on as a partner.

They always gracefully declined but promised they would consider his proposals anytime he was interested. Nick loved to entertain him when he dropped by.

The wedding would be a simple affair. The group of thirty or so family members would gather tomorrow for the rehearsal, and they were an active and fun bunch of people. The wedding would be populated with lots of people he knew from SEAL Team 3, and Nick was looking forward to it.

THE WEDDING HAPPENED on a bright, sunny day that briefly started out with a light rain, which Nick was actually grateful for because it tamped down all the dust on the roads and leaves and soaked into the soil so that it gave everything a crisp and fresh-washed look. The vineyard glistened. It was almost as if God put a water hose to his garden and cleaned it up for butterflies, birds, and humans to enjoy.

Kyle Lansdowne, his former LPO, attended, as well as several others from the team. He caught up on some of the team stories, including new weddings and births. Armando's wife, Gina, had passed, and his new marriage thrived. Several other pieces of news filtered in, and he found himself able to listen without feeling like he had missed something. It had taken him many years to get used to not being on that team or not being available whenever they called. But he didn't owe them that obligation any longer.

Kyle walked up to him and shook his hand.

Nicholas had to give him a pile of crap for that. "So

we're hand shaking now, like business people? Not that good old man slap? What happened to that?" Nicholas asked him.

"Oh hell, Nicholas, guilty as charged," Kyle said as he grabbed him around the shoulders, gave him a quick hug, and then slapped him on the back three almost-vertebrae-cracking times. "There you go, Son. That better?"

"Exactly. Glad I asked. Now when my back ribs heal, I'll be happy again," Nicholas said.

Kyle warmed him with a smile. "You know, I look around here at this beautiful place, and I remember when we were getting it ready to sell for Sophie. What you've done with it?" He shook his head. "I mean, it's just magical. It's such a beautiful place. And I'm glad to see that it's not just a gentleman's hobby. You're actually making good money here. I like that," Kyle said.

"Well, I appreciate that. I mean, you guys all invested in Frog Haven up in Healdsburg. You guys knew all about the winery business for years before we got involved in this one. I'm glad we could do it on our own. And I'm grateful for all the investors that have come our way since."

"You earned it, Nick. You and Devon have worked your butts off. And raised three beautiful girls in the process, too."

"Thanks, Landmine," Nick said, using the nickname Kyle had earned while they served together. It brought a smile to his former LPO's face. "But honestly, Kyle, I was just thinking a couple of days ago I was made for this. I mean, this is the life I wanted to lead."

"Now you sound like Brady. I never would've thought that big old tatted guy with all the scars and crap all over his body would turn into a farmer of butterflies, papayas, and bananas of all things. Could you believe it?"

"Yeah, I can. He's got Maggie; he's got Emma; he's got it all. I feel the same way. There is nothing light about running a business like a winery or a wedding center or a lavender farm. It's a lot of darn work. You're outside in the sun a lot, and you go to bed exhausted, but it's a good life."

"You wear it well, Farmer Nick."

"We've got lots of future plans. As a tourist destination, we're going to build some little guest cottages over there, and I think it'll be even better. And there's a lot of people who would like to be a winery owner for a week, but they can't handle the financial obligation and all the work it takes to own one full time. But they like the experience of it. So we're going to give that to them."

"Brilliant. But I think you *must* be talking to Brady, because that's what he's saying too."

"We talk all the time, compare notes and share ideas. Brady's happy. He's got what he wants. And I have what I want. It's perfect. I mean, I never thought I'd find the perfect life, and I have."

Kyle slapped him on the back again, this time more gently.

"Good for you, Nick. I'm really seriously happy for you."

The cleanup ladies came in after the wedding reception was over. The moon was starting to set, and Nick and Devon took the girls and went to bed while the cleanup crew was still working. He knew they would continue until one or two o'clock in the morning, wiping down all the floors and windows, sanitizing the kitchen prep area and the restrooms, sweeping everything, and then carting all the linens and extra tables and chairs away to be washed in a different location.

The cleanup crew was quiet, but Nick still couldn't sleep. He heard crickets, sort of early for this time of year, early summer. He listened to their songs and thought about Sophie hearing noises on the outside, animals and such.

He got up and, after checking to see that Devon was asleep, took his flashlight and made a perimeter walk around the house. He checked Sophie's window and confirmed that it was still firmly locked. The reception area and the pavilion was clean and devoid of all the crew who had left probably not more than a half hour ago. It smelled fresh and sanitized. They'd left the windows open so the breeze could dry the floors and the windows and all the other washed surfaces.

He took a chair from inside and placed it outside under the overhang in front of the double doors at the pavilion entrance. Looking at the night sky, listening to the crickets, he was truly as content as he'd ever been.

He'd always made it a habit of bringing his cell phone with them, an old habit from his Team days. On his way back to the bedroom, it buzzed in his back pocket. He pulled it out and noticed it was a phone number for Winston Harris, his real estate attorney.

He answered the phone with, "Winston, what the hell are you doing at one o'clock in the morning?"

"I couldn't sleep."

"Well, that makes two of us, Winston. So what's up? Is there a problem?"

"There's no easy way to say this, Nicholas, but I got some real bad news."

Nicholas clenched his fists and gritted his teeth, setting his jaw square for news he wasn't going to like.

"Go ahead," he sighed.

"Well, Enemario Rodriguez was released today. Apparently, there was some kind of an irregularity with the way he was charged, which affects his case. He may have to go through another trial, but his time served is ended."

"But he was only gone… what? Eight years? Eight years of a thirty-five-years-to-life sentence? That doesn't make sense, Winston."

"Agreed. Full with you there, one hundred percent. They're going back through and looking at all the cases, especially where there was a minority defendant, especially in murder charges. It's a apwxiL project, a grant they received from the federal government to look into these cases. And they found some charging errors the judge apparently made at sentencing. So they're tossing the case. Doesn't mean he can't be retried, but he's out. You know how much the Sonoma County D.A. loves to re-try old cases she didn't handle in the first place."

"Fuck sake, Winston. That's just bullshit, and you know it." Nick felt his blood boil.

"I agree. Anyway, he's going to be out, and they can't hold him for the new trial, because he's served more than eight years, and apparently, that's the rule."

"So you mean he's out now or going to be? Like, he's free? He's walking around, free as a bird. He could be over here now."

"I was told that he went back to Mexico, but he hasn't been deported and he hasn't lost his passport. He's a free man, Nicholas. It sucks to high heaven. But

Enemario Rodriguez is now back in the picture. And I'd be a fool if I didn't tell you... you better get ready for another war."

CHAPTER 2

DEVON AND NICHOLAS met with their attorney early the next morning.

"He can't really do that, can he? I mean, he can't come after us! Wouldn't everybody be looking at them? Wouldn't he be somebody of interest if anything should happen to any one of us?" Devon asked.

Nick knew evil lived everywhere, and just because something wasn't a good idea didn't mean bad actors wouldn't try to do it. He was not happy with the news, and it was still settling in on exactly what his options were. In his dealings with warlords in Africa and some of the men he had to confront in the Middle East, he knew they'd go down fighting, no matter the cost to them, their families, or their fellow countrymen. But evil was a whole lot less predictable than good. He and his team buddies were always a force for good. Good was more predictable. That was the huge problem. The enemy always could guess where and when they'd strike, because on the Teams, they tried to protect innocent life. The enemy used that "weakness" or Achilles' heel to their advantage.

Harris quickly remarked, "Nick, I'm going to let you explain to your wife why that is a logical idea, but something that doesn't hold up when you're talking about bad guys. Or am I wrong?"

"I was just thinking the same thing." Nick turned to Devon. "I'm afraid, Devon, that this guy was willing to murder to get what he wanted. Sophie paid the price until we got wise to him and caught him fair and square. I'm thinking he's lost quite a bit, unless he's got some infusion of capital coming in from somewhere, but with the winery in disrepair—nobody running it, nobody doing anything about it, and everybody in the family fighting for it, according to our neighbor here— I'm thinking he's just a desperate man. And desperate men do crazy, stupid, awful things."

Nick waited to let that sink in a bit. Then he added, "We're going to have to institute some procedures at the house and talk to the girls about safety. But this guy will have to be stopped, by us or law enforcement, because I don't think he has the balls to quit on his own or realize he's a lost cause. I don't want to say too much, but there may come a time we'll have to defend ourselves physically."

Devon was already nodding her head before he'd

finished. "Nick, I get it. And I know you're probably not telling me everything you're worried about or suspecting either." She examined her hands wringing in her lap, and then she tossed a hard stare at the attorney. "Is there anything we can do to look into how he was released and how the order came through? I mean, do you understand these types of things or should we hire someone who can intercede and perhaps set straight what was done, in my opinion, wrongly?"

Harris took a deep breath and studied the view from his upper floor window. "It's the political climate, Devon. It's just not going to be something that's easy. I wish I could promise you a good result. I would be the first one to refer you to a good federal attorney who has prosecuted and defended cases like this, because this now *is* federal since he was granted a stay, basically, and released without any input from the local district attorney or the victims. That's you and Nick. This is a very unusual and special situation. Somebody very high up is pulling the strings on this one. I just don't think there's anyone out there who would be worth the money you would spend trying to fight it. But I can look into it if you want."

Nick inserted another thought. "Devon, they have a lot of money behind them. They've got a federal grant, and with that comes the charge that they get people out of prison who've been wrongly convicted. It's a very popular idea, and of course, there are people in prison who don't belong there. Yes, our legal system is flawed. But this is funded by a non-profit based on these federal grants, plus contributions from people who believe in that theory. In the process, unfortunately, there are some real bad actors who are going to be let loose. And that's because we are living in the times we are living in. I think we're going to have to be careful and watchful. It's a David and Goliath thing. I'm not going to fight the federal government, but I will do what I can physically to protect our family."

"Tell your SEAL buddies. Nick, let them know please."

"I'm going to have to be careful, because they can't really intercede, but—"

"Oh, come on. When Zak was having trouble, when Jameson was having trouble... we've had several people who you guys came to their aid when they needed it. Even Christy Lansdowne, when she was kidnapped, remember? Those guys would do anything for you, Nick. You could call them in."

"Agreed. But I don't want to get them in trouble."

Harris gave the last response. "Why don't you give them a call, Nicholas? Let's let them be the decider of that. And I'm telling you right here and now, don't be thinking any violence. The guy is just playing out his rights. You don't want to violate yours or your family's by doing something stupid. So we have to be careful. But I'd tell your buddies. And let them make the decision."

Nick and Devon didn't say much on the way home. His mind was playing over and over again the events that had occurred, the trial of Rodriguez, relief when he was sent away, and now the impending steps he was going to have to take to make sure his family was safe.

He knew seeking revenge or doing anything that would harm Rodriguez would be a certain trip to prison, and if any of his buddies helped him, they'd lose their Trident. But his mind went to all those devious places—could he off the guy and somehow get rid of the body so that nobody knew about it? He knew in his heart of hearts that Rodriguez was so dirty and so dangerous that the only way to stop him was to kill him.

But that went against everything he had done as a SEAL. It crossed the lines of decency, and it wasn't the type of thing an honorable man would do, even though fully justified. It just wasn't something he'd be able to go that far with. Not unless he caught Rodriguez in the act. And he hoped and prayed he'd be able to get there in time or respond quickly enough.

Devon was eyeing him, and he knew when she did that she was worried about what was going on in his mind. There was no way in the world he was going to tell her.

Finally, he met her gaze. They were headed off the freeway onto Bennett Valley Road, not more than about five minutes from their home.

"Nick, I know I have in the past worried about some of the things that happened to you when you were overseas, and I know there are limits to what you can and cannot do. I also know you so well I can tell you're considering doing some unspeakable, unthinkable things. I'm not trained, and we do live by a moral code, and you're aware of that. I've always trusted you to do the right thing. I trust you today as well as I did at the very first when I fell in love with you. But please promise me you won't put yourself in jeopardy, even if you think it's going to help me and the girls. I know where your heart is, sweetheart. But I don't want to live here and live on this planet with something having happened to you. Especially because you were protecting us. I wouldn't be able to carry on. And then he'd win."

Nick kept his eyes on the road but felt moisture gather then run down his cheeks. He was moved by Devon's little reveal.

"I was trained to protect the innocent. I will always do that, Devon."

He wanted to phrase his words carefully. It was important she understand some of what he was thinking but not all of it. He continued, "We were trained to go in and protect people who never knew our names, who didn't care one bit about us, who in fact, in many cases, hated our guts. But we still kept them safe. Now, when it comes to protecting you and the girls, yes, I'm on board with that. All of us are. But we have laws and rules here. Other countries do as well, but we are tasked with intervention. We are invited in. We're given permission to act in those cases with deadly force, or we don't go. In our own country, it's not our jurisdiction. *We're* not protected. And the bottom line is nobody can protect us like our community can. That's very hard to wait and watch and leave the task of removing criminals from the population here in the United States up to local police, sheriff, and FBI. They have more constraints on them than we ever did. But that doesn't mean we can take the law into our own hands."

"So what are you thinking?"

"I'm just thinking, Devon. I'm going to train you guys to observe. Even Sophia needs to be aware. I'm going to try to do it in a way that doesn't scare the girls, especially her. I think there are some things we can put into place for our own safety, things I never thought I'd have to do again."

"When will this plan go into effect?" she asked.

"Like yesterday. But I still need to sort all this out, and I need some advice. I can't very well ask someone from the Sonoma County Sheriff's Office what they think, because then I'll be exposing myself as a suspect if something should befall Rodriguez. I hesitate to get my fellow former teammates involved—"

"But what about the group that Tucker knows, that group of people the guy you know from Portland is setting up?"

"Oh, you mean Colin Riley and his group?"

"Yes. Weren't they working on some kind of a paramilitary group to help protect and do things that perhaps locals couldn't do? Was that what they were talking about?"

"More for outside the country, honey. We still have to be very careful inside the United States' border. It's frustrating, I know, and most people don't understand. We don't really want a trained army going after our own citizens. That's a very dangerous place to go. Doesn't take much to imagine what would happen if we had a rogue politician or political party that justified the use of a militia to go after our own citizens. We have years of precedent on that and years of mistakes, but we're getting better, I'd like to think. We don't want to throw out the Constitution just because we have one bad guy we want to get. What happens when the person is unjustly accused? Has defenders? Do we go after them? And when and how would we ever know when it's all left up to the whim of someone in power who could be flawed, delusional, or, worse, working for a foreign enemy? We're talking takeover of the United States. I cannot be a part of that."

"I get it. No. Not worth one bad guy to do that. But somehow there has to be a way, Nick."

"We can't have vigilante justice right and left. It interferes with our democratic process, as slow and laborious as it is. It's fraught with fraud just like any other country out there. We're no different. No, there will be an answer that'll come to me. I just don't have it right now. And thank you for your trust. That means a lot to me."

She reached over and took Nick's hand then brought it up to her lips and kissed the underside of his hand, his palm, just like he often did to her.

"I know you'll find the right solution, Nick. I had to say my piece just so you know, to reinforce some of the things you and I have discussed. I understand these past four years have been perhaps an anomaly. Maybe that's why you've loved this time together, this building of this happy place. Being constructive is what you were made for, not tearing down governments or hunting down and killing people. You are a man who likes to build, and we're building a legacy here. I would like nothing more than to continue celebrating happy events, luncheons, weddings, receptions, and parties. Celebrations of every kind. There's something wonderful about creating a stage, a place for all that to occur. And I'm not naïve. I know that freedom has to be protected, and it's very fragile."

"It is, Devon. You absolutely got it one hundred percent right. Freedom is so fragile, and we are so lucky to have it. Nothing good comes of violence. And I say that as a sometimes-violent man. But we as SEALs are trained to address those people that you guys, everybody here in this country, don't have to deal with. It hurts my heart when I see it happening here. And although it might be frustrating, don't confuse my frustration for a lack of ability or inability to solve it. I am going to solve it."

She nodded.

"I will come up with a solution. I just can't tell you right now what that is. And I also want to tell you there may be parts of this you may never know about. One thing is for sure, though. I won't do anything that will jeopardize our situation. Our situation is worth fighting for. And if someone comes after us, they are going to be dealt with one way or another. I hope that our friends in law enforcement help us out on that score. But if not, I'm not about to see my wife and children terrorized by somebody who's pure evil. There's no way we can live next door to a person like that. It's like dealing with the devil himself. He takes, and you give, and he takes, and you give, and he takes, and then he eventually overruns everything. Because he's stupid and strong. He's full of vibrato and hubris. He doesn't think. He doesn't care about anything or anyone but himself. He's so self-obsessed that it's an opportunity for us, a blind spot he may not notice until it's too late. We're not like him."

Devon squeezed his hand and said, "But we do care. We do."

CHAPTER 3

NICK DECIDED TO alert Zak and Amy to their situation. He drove up to Healdsburg, turning at the sign for Frog Haven winery. Amy greeted him on the front porch of their house carrying a basket of flowers.

"Welcome, Stranger. This must really be important," she said.

Nick parked his Hummer and got out, giving Amy a kiss on the cheek.

"Here, let me take these in for you," he said as he grabbed the basket of flowers. He buried his nose in the middle of them. "These smell lovely. Devon does the same thing."

"I'll bet she does, Sailor. How's everything going there?" Amy asked. She opened the front door, leading him into their living room and crossing it. Then she motioned for him to set the basket on the island counter in the kitchen.

"You guys remodeled in here, right?" Nick said, studying the cabinets.

"Yeah, new countertops and repainted the wood cabinets. I decided a little light gray was a better color for me. I've kind of gotten tired of dark oak colors now that, you know, we see so much out in the vineyard of all these different colors. I just wanted something lighter and cleaner looking."

"Looks great. And I love the granite."

"I would've opted for tile, which was cheaper, but Zak was right. Solid slab stone is the best way to go."

"And I bet it's easier for making pies and preparing food for the winery visitor center," Nick said.

"You got that right."

She started sorting the flowers, separating the sweet peas from the roses and the Brown-Eyed Susans from the snap dragons and stock plants. She was intent on her arranging, but it didn't take long before her old question resurfaced.

"You didn't answer my question. How are things going? Or should I ask to what do I owe this visit?"

Nick knew a pure social call would require him to bring Devon and the girls and would necessitate a phone call first. Nick also understood that all of the SEALs and former SEALs were hesitant to say too much on the telephone for fear of getting caught up in some kind of random surveillance. Although none of them felt they were being targets of such, they were careful. Just in case.

Good girl, he thought.

"I never could get anything over on you, could I, Amy?"

"Well, in farming, ranching, and the tourist industry, there are good months and bad months. There are good years and bad years. It's the nature of the business. There's always something coming up. New taxes, new regulations… and I want to think that it's for the public good, but oftentimes, it's just more red tape we have to deal with. I'm hoping it's something simple like that." She ended her statement by peering directly into his eyes.

Nick knew he should wait and talk to Zak first, but he just couldn't keep a secret from Amy.

"Enemario Rodriguez has been released from prison. They found some issues with his charging orders given by the judge at his sentencing, and it's reversed his conviction. He's not an innocent man. He's just a man who's had his sentence reversed. So he's free."

He watched as the gray clouds covered her eyes, as her brow furrowed, as her lips turned down in sad contemplation of the news.

"Zak is going to be really upset to hear this. Is there anything you can do? Or is there something *we* can do somehow?"

"No, not at the moment. We're getting geared up for a potential re-escalation of the problems between us. He still owns the property next door, although it's gone into complete disrepair."

"Why don't we just all go together and buy him out, like give him way more money than it's worth, just to get rid of him. Wouldn't that be the best way to treat him?"

"Only if he really needs money. He's not acting like he does, or he never did. Maybe now he does. But I honestly don't know what his motives are, and he's not going to get our property. I mean, he ought to know by now there isn't anything he can do that would make me sell to him or deed over my—our farm to him."

"I get that loud and clear, Nick."

"And you would think a person like that would want to operate in some part of Sonoma county where he could sort of do his own thing and not be watched. But he's smack dab in the middle of Bennett Valley where houses and subdivisions with multimillion dollar price tags look straight down on him. Once they find out, they're going to have a hard time knowing a murderer is operating some kind of criminal enterprise down there."

"We hope the public would object. You're worried it won't help, right? They don't really have the power do they?"

"Yeah, that's my concern. I just came to talk it over with Zak and see what he thought. I need some ideas. I'm in the fact-finding phase. And then I've got to throw myself into security for our house and the business. I've got to train the girls, even Sophia."

"Sophia, she's so cute. How old is she now?"

"She's almost four. Got a birthday coming up. A very precocious four. Taking after her auntie."

"I would expect nothing less."

Amy messaged Zak, who was out working in the vineyards, and he texted back he would be back into the house in about fifteen to twenty minutes.

"You want some coffee?" she asked.

"Love some, Amy. Thanks."

"So how *is* your business then? I hear it's just booming."

"We've had a record year so far. I was recently feeling so peaceful and so grateful for everything. And now this. But I guess these sorts of things come up all the time. If it's not a problem with a neighbor, it could be finances or taxes or health. You know, the cycle you mentioned."

"Don't I know it, Nick. With Zak's eye injury, he wanted so much to be on the teams. And he tried so hard to re-qualify, and technically, he did. But at the last minute, they scratched him. That broke his heart, and I almost thought it would break his spirit too. He had to work that one through, and I almost lost him there. So I understand. I think we're given challenges. My grandfather used to say we never get lessons that are too strong, that God knows what our limits are. I think he was right."

"I think the lesson in all of this is that you appreciate what you have. You don't envy what you don't have, and—" Nick was at a loss for words.

Amy inserted what he needed to hear. "You protect what you've got, and you make it last forever. You build a dynasty, like you are. Like we are. You protect it, you let it flourish, expand. There's one thing I've learned from the ups and downs of this business. It's that good is stronger than evil. I wish we didn't have to battle it so much. But you know, I think we enjoy it a lot more because it isn't easy, is it?"

"No, it sure isn't."

"What's not easy? You making moves on my wife, Nick?" Zak said as he wandered in through the back door of the kitchen. He washed his hands in the sink and then reached over and gave Nick a bear hug.

"Nah, I'm not making moves on Amy. She's squarely in your corner, man. Besides, I kind of have a nice one at home myself."

"Yes, you do. So let's get down to business or has Amy pulled all of your secrets out of you yet?"

"Can we go in the other room and sit down for a

bit? I have some, well, it's some tough news."

"Enemario Rodriguez has been released from prison, Zak," Amy whispered.

"Holy shit. Goddamn it. I thought that cretin was put away forever. Didn't they say he'd never get out? Or he wouldn't live long enough to get out?" Zak asked.

"That's the criminal justice system for you. Always someone out there making sure everybody did the right thing. In this case, a nonprofit group took on the case, and, well, they found some errors, so the judgment got tossed. You know, if it was done incorrectly, then I'm on the side of the fence that says okay, those things shouldn't happen in our country. I'm sympathetic to that. But goddamn it, this guy out on the street after what he did? I just don't see how anybody could rule in his favor."

"They must have found something big. They must have found the judge made a huge mistake of some kind. I don't understand it, and I don't want to. Let's sit down and talk about it. You tell me your thoughts, Nick."

The two of them walked into the living room. Amy called after Zak, "You want a coffee, Zak? I'm making some for Nick."

Zak looked at Nick and then looked at his wife and then looked at Nick again.

"I need some Bourbon for this conversation. I think I'm going to need some alcohol, not caffeine. I need the wisdom of some good Kentucky bourbon."

"Well, if I wasn't driving a half an hour south on the freeway, I'd join you. But I just can't help following the rules," Nick said.

"Amen to that. Okay, she'll make your coffee, but let's sit down over here and solve the problems of the world, shall we?"

Nick spent two hours in serious discussion with Zak. They came up with several scenarios and choices, and some of it was based on information they had about Mr. Rodriguez and his former tactics. Nick mentioned what Amy had brought up about buying him out, and Zak was intrigued with that.

"Gosh, I think we could raise several million dollars. I don't know what he wants for the place, but with no water, the logical thing would be to connect it to your property and use your water. It's just that we don't know if that's what he wants, right?" Zak asked.

"That's exactly what I was thinking, too, and worried about. But as much as we don't think it would work, I still think we should try. I'm for a nonviolent, peaceful resolution. I know one thing, though. There's no reasoning with him. I don't think the man understands logic. He's got this bravado in him that is just all consuming. I mean, why kill somebody because you want to take over their water? What kind of a person does that?" Nick asked.

"Someone who doesn't have a soul."

"My sister really didn't like him and didn't ever hold back her contempt. She sure sparked a fire. I think this guy became obsessed with doing her in, sorry to say."

"But was there any reasonable way to deal with him?" Zak asked.

"Probably not, dammit."

"Don't blame Sophie. It wasn't her fault. She was a fighter, and she felt threatened by his overtures to buy the land, especially when he knew she was having financial trouble. He was an opportunist, and Sophie knew that was the sign of a morally corrupt individual. She called it like it was." Zak shrugged.

While Nick finished his coffee, Zak finished off his tumbler, leaving the large ice cube half melted in the middle. They both stared at the melting piece of ice, as if there were answers there.

"You know, Nick, I think you ought to talk to the guys. I know you're probably hesitant to, but don't you think they should know?"

"I don't want any white knights here, Zak."

"Oh, so you think they'll just, you know, let your wife and kids and you handle this on your own? You really think they'd do that, Nick?"

"Nah, you're right. But I don't want vigilante justice."

"No, you want effective protection. You and I both

know there's really only one permanent solution."

"Don't say it, Zak. Please don't say it. We know what that is. But I don't want to go there. I don't want to get involved in that."

"Some of the guys are going to think—"

Nick interrupted him. "It's not their fight, Zak. It's *my* decision. I don't want the responsibility of telling them this is what I want to do. I don't want to get them involved. If it ever came to that, though, you bet I tell them."

"I still think you should talk to them. Kyle, at least. What about Mark Beale? Maybe somebody knows somebody who can look into this nonprofit organization. Somebody who can counteract what they're doing."

"I asked my attorney about that, and he's pretty connected, but that's a long fight and years and years of struggle, not to mention the cost. The danger to my family with him being loose is immediate. I can't wait for something to happen legally, and I can't do anything illegal, so I have to do something smart."

"So you need to get prepared."

The two men looked at each other and nodded in unison.

"I'm making a list, Zak. Devon's a pretty good shot, but we're going to step up the firearms training. I'm going to show the girls some simple things, and I'm going to get an alarm system installed."

"Those are good steps. Those are logical steps. But I also want you to call Kyle and ask him about telling the guys. You know we all came over and worked on that place. We all met Sophie, and we shared the grief when she passed away. There's just something wrong about this guy coming back on the scene, maybe taking what he tried to get before. Sophie's not the enemy now. You are," said Zak.

"Roger that," Nick mumbled. "You know we always used to talk about not underestimating the enemy."

"Oh, *that* guy, the enemy. The evil one."

"And I told Devon that the evil ones are unpredictable. That's the hard part about all this. I can't retaliate until he makes an action. So he gets the first bite? He gets to make the first move. And then we have to beat his force with an appropriate reaction. But I also have to make it so that I'm prepared for every scenario, so that we are not living in a prison of our own house because we're afraid to go outside and confront him. We still have our life, our business, our center, but we have to be smart about how we do it. I'm not about to close down just to be safe."

"Well, like I said, there's one way to cure it for sure. If you run out of all options, I could still do it, Nick. But don't you dare tell my wife I said that."

CHAPTER 4

NICK REACHED OUT to Mark Beale, who had been his roommate throughout Great Lakes and had been one of his best buddies when he was serving on the teams. Mark had come up with Nick when they were talking to Sophie about selling her property and arranging for her final affairs. And for a brief period of time, Mark had a very low-key fling with his sister shortly before she died.

Now a happily married man and father of two, Mark coincidentally married a woman named Sophia. But it was just a coincidence. She was a dancer on a cruise ship several team guys and their wives went on, and since Nick couldn't go, he'd had to relive the experience through Mark's illustrious storytelling. When the ship was taken over by terrorists, it turned out to be quite an adventure.

Mark settled in the San Diego area and was still messing with the idea of getting off the teams, something he'd been doing for several years. But he and Sophia needed to buy a bigger house, so he re-upped after six years for the re-enlistment bonus.

"So how long are you in for this time, Mark?" Nick asked him when he reached him on the phone.

"Not enough time to get the mortgage paid off on this thing. Boy, did we buy at the wrong time. Prices have come down, and Sophia's still getting pregnant. We're going to have another one now, so that makes three."

"Well, I've got three. It's no big deal. It's just an extra bed and a lot of extra family time. I think you're not going to notice it until they're older and they start playing baseball and soccer and whatever the hell else they'll do down there. I think it's a good sign, Mark."

"Everything is so expensive, even as it goes down. If we sold this house to try to get something bigger, I would have to go an hour and a half outside of San Diego County. I'd be spending all my time on the freeway, whereas this way, Sophia has to work in the dance studio so we can make ends meet. I, of course, work too, and then she has to stop dancing when I'm on deployment to take care of the kids. You didn't call to hear my shit, Nick. So what's up?"

"Well, I don't want to talk about it too much on the phone, but I just want you to know that Enemario Rodriguez is out of prison. His conviction is being tossed. One of those cases where they go in and make sure there were no charging errors, and apparently, there were. I'd like to strangle the group that did it, but if it was done wrong, even if he's a bad guy, we do the right thing in this country, right?"

"Bullshit!" It was Mark's favorite word.

"Well, I need some advice. And maybe I'll just come down there and talk to a few of you guys. I don't really want to do it over the phone. On the other hand, I don't want to leave Devon and the girls all alone."

"Can't you get some guys to stand in for you while you're gone? Shit, Nick, I can't go up there. We're working up to the deployment, doing a lot of extra training. I just can't do it. And if I leave Sophia with the girls, her being pregnant, I might come home and find she's taken off with some guy from Brazil and taken the girls with her."

"Funny." Nick knew Sophia was engaged to a Brazilian dancer at one time.

"Not. Not at all. Can you come down here?"

Nick thought about it before answering. "When do you deploy?"

"We're going up to Alaska for another training, God help us. Do you know how much snow and ice you find in West Africa?"

"Well, who knows? Maybe they take a detour, and you'll wind up in Russia or someplace."

"Hardly. And the last time I checked, they don't have walruses or porpoises or whales in Africa, either, so I don't know what the hell they're doing. We're going to be practicing with—well, you know the drill—Jeeps, 50-cals, target practice at sixty miles an hour. You were there. You did it."

"Wonder why they're not doing it in the desert?"

"Beats me. Maybe they figured nobody would see us there. I don't know. Anyway, next week, we go there. Then the following week, we're off, and then we're locked down for ten days before deployment. I got to get some shots. I got to stay quarantined, sort of. They've got some nasty stuff going on over there, and I don't want to bring it home."

"I got you. So how does that work?" Nick asked.

"We're all supposed to quarantine and only see members of the team and their families. That means Sophia has to do all the shopping, and I stay home except for my workouts. It's the way it is. Things are changing. Things are getting very dangerous too."

Nick was more grateful than ever that he was no longer on the team. But he appreciated the commitment Mark made. He was in awe of not only what Mark did today but what they both did just ten years ago.

"I think that's good timing. You go on up to Alaska and target practice on some walruses or icebergs. I'm going to do a few things here that I have to do first, and I'll see if I can arrange for somebody to stand in for the family. I'll come down there the beginning of the following week, and be done before you have to go into quarantine. Does that work?"

"Absolutely. It'll be great to see you, Nick. How is the family otherwise?"

"Well, up until a couple of days ago, I would have told you everything was hunky-dory, A-OK, super Roger that. But, with this news, we're a little spooked. The girls are having a great time here, and little Sophia… you haven't seen her yet, have you?"

"Nope. And you haven't seen any of mine."

"Can I hang with you at your house or—?"

"Sure as hell you can. But you're probably going to get the dog on the couch on top of you. Maybe the baby will come wandering in and want to cuddle. When you've got two in diapers at once, it's just crazy. So, as long as you don't mind us having to get up in the middle of the night and change a diaper or get some food or something for them and you don't mind the crying, you're more than welcome. And if not, well, then you can sleep in your truck."

"I still got the Hummer. I might do that."

"You asshole. No, you're not going to sleep in your Hummer. You're going to sleep in my house. It might be on the living room couch, but you're going to sleep in my house. It's been too long, my friend."

"Okay. I'll text you my ETA, and you let me know if anything changes."

Nicholas was happy to have the little smack talk conversation. He'd forgotten how much he missed it. He remembered coming back to town after his first trainings and deployment and talking to his friends, who commented about how every other word he told them was a swear word. It was one of those things that all young tadpoles got into. They went away to school and for training as bright, respectful eighteen to twenty-one-year-old kids then come home swearing like a sailor or a Merchant Marine. But it was funny how easily he snuck back into that life. He wondered in the back of his mind whether he was really done with that service. But he knew he was.

Nick arranged to have a security company recommended to him by several of his friends come over and wire up the house, add extra sensors to the gates and fencing around their property, and install cameras and devices so he could be alerted. He knew it was going to drive him batty, especially since they had coyotes, wild turkeys, birds of every kind, ferrets, skunks, raccoons, rats, and gophers running across the land nearly 24-7. The larger animals like the coyotes were the ones that would mess up the fencing. The deer population could almost smell the electric fences, so he didn't worry too much about them, and they were very docile. But the coyotes, almost legendary for being able to climb wire fences, would be the biggest problem and would probably make him tear all his remaining hair out.

The wiring was completed in two days, and they had a dedicated computer for the purpose of recording all the cameras, the signals, and the perimeter alerts. The computer would download all the material every night to both his and Devon's computers, as well as a backup that was somewhere near downtown Santa Rosa on a separate server.

The technicians who installed it explained how everything worked, even showed the girls how to arm and disarm the doors, and made them trip the alarm several times so they got used to the sound of the blast. The first time it happened all three girls burst into tears and ran for their mother.

Nick explained to the whole family there was the possibility a very bad man was going to be moving in next door at the vineyard and that it was necessary to take these steps to keep everybody safe. He also expressed to them the fact that if they didn't pay attention, even when they thought they didn't have to, they might be caught off guard and people who do bad things sometimes take advantage of that situation.

"He might watch. He might use night scopes or binoculars to track what you do outside in the night or the day. He might even peer into your windows. We've put sensors on all the windows, and we're going to make it so that when you pull the screen down, no one can see what's going on in the room, so you will have some semblance of privacy. But once you go outside, girls, all bets are off. The perimeter fencing will be wired, and cameras and lights will come on, but there won't be anything to protect you if somebody happens to breach the fence."

All three girls looked at him with wide brown eyes. He knew they were scared to death.

Nick softened his tone and explained further. "I know it's asking an awful lot of you three to not be afraid. I'm asking you to be brave. And here's why you have to be brave. If you get scared, you're going to think about all kinds of bad things, and that's going to take your eye off doing what you have to do to keep yourself safe. So remember, even if you're afraid, you have to do what we've talked about. You have to take care of yourself and your sisters and your mother, and you have to make sure that you get word to someone who can help you, whether that's me or your mother or one of the hands in the field or perhaps some of the other people I'm going to have coming over to help out. You need to try to keep yourself calm and breathe."

Over the next days, he showed them how to do box

breathing, how to look at everything in the room and observe everything they could without missing any detail. He did drills with them, putting objects on a tray and asking them to memorize all the things on that tray, so that they could increase their recall if something should happen and they were asked to recreate it. He asked them questions like what was the color of the dustpan in the closet in the kitchen or what color were the bristles on the broom. He asked them what color was the towel they used last night before they went to bed. He was always springing little questions and little tests of their memory.

Nick found that the more he did this, the more it became like a game. And he also discovered the girls worked quicker and quicker to assume what they needed to do to become observant, such as start looking at their circumstances or watching cars or counting cars or giving each other questions. He heard the girls asking each other what was the color of the last car they passed on the road? What was the color of the store clerk's glasses?

It was a family project created to help or assist in the savings of their lives.

He and Devon went target-practicing every day, down at the gun range. He had Devon shoot his 9 mm, and he got her a snub nose .45 that was lightweight enough for her to feel comfortable in the palm of her hand. He even showed her how to use a shotgun, which she didn't like at all. But he wanted her to get comfortable with the sound of the blast in case she had to use his.

"Aren't I supposed to know how to take my weapon apart and put it back together again?" Devon asked him one day.

"No, I don't think so. I'm going to handle all of that. But you do have to be comfortable with the sound, the kick, and how you sight it. You have to learn to load it. You don't want to be putting in the wrong size ammunition or scrambling to find the ammunition. You know these are all important things. If you don't know how to handle this or don't know how to find what you need, you won't be able to use deadly force if you should have to."

"I kind of liked it when I was using the baseball bat. Last time I came up against Rodriguez, I was wielding that thing, and—"

"Yeah, you knocked the hell out of him, and you knocked the hell out of me too."

"Well, I'm going to still practice with my baseball bat. Now that the girls are playing softball, we're going to have a whole bunch of those all over the house."

"That's a good idea, Devon. Show them how to smash pumpkins and apples. You show them how to hit a tree and not fall down from the kickback, okay?"

"I guess I'm going to be investing in some new bats then. Is that what you're saying?"

He removed the weapon from her hand, made sure the safety was on, and placed it on the table in front of them. He grabbed her and pulled her to his chest. "Sweetheart, I wouldn't care if you bought fifty bats. It wouldn't bother me one bit. I just want you guys to look like sweet innocent women and know, if you had to, how to kill a man. Because if you are to defend our girls, if it comes to that, you don't pick up that gun unless you're going to cause a death. That's the way you've got to look at it. You don't pick it up to scare them away. You pick it up to shoot it and to kill."

One evening, Nick and Devon also hosted Amy and Zak and their girls, showing them around the property and, in particular, showing them the defense system they'd set up. Amy was all in favor of doing this at Frog Haven as well.

"It sort of feels like a prison sometimes," Devon started, "but then I have to remember, like Nick told me, the evil ones never do the predictable things. I'm trying to be less predictable myself by being ready for whatever happens… that's the unpredictable part or the part of us that he might underestimate."

Amy shook her head from side to side. "Underestimate you guys at his own peril. Maybe that would be threat enough."

Zak was quick to correct her. "No. No, he's got to be totally surprised. When he sees you guys can fight, and it's not as easy as he thought, he's going to have that oh shit moment and rethink his strategy. That gives you enough time to either get away or cause some kind of damage so that he will be captured."

Nick agreed. "That's the way we're looking at it. We're looking at it like a project, like a game, but like any good baseball game, we play for keeps. We play to win."

"We play to survive," Devon said. "So much of the world is in survival mode anyway. We've never had to do this, and it was only a matter of time before some of this crossed our path. Better to be prepared and never need it than to be unprepared and have your life taken away or, worse, have one of our girls fall prey to him. I'm going to fight for everything I've got. And I think I'm really going to enjoy it."

Zak, Amy, and Nick all looked at her incredulously. But it was Nick who spoke up first. "Sweetheart, I have no doubt that, once you get started, it might be kind of hard to get you to stop."

Zak laughed. "You know they have those survivalist camps where they give you a little bit of jerky, some water, and a KA-BAR-like knife and a hatchet—one of those special-made hatchets. You have to go out and wander through the wilderness, and if you don't come back in two days, they come get you. You have to kill your own food and find water and shelter, and it's that survivalist experience that most people aren't attracted to. But, Devon, I think you could even do one of those TV programs. Wouldn't that be something, Devon on Survivor?"

Amy shook her head. "No. I'd rather see her making pies, combing the girls' hair, and sitting down by the fireplace. Or dancing or singing. They're only learning to do this so they get to do that a lot more. She doesn't need to become a survivalist. She just needs to be turned from aluminum to steel."

CHAPTER 5

NICK SLUNG HIS duffel bag over his shoulder, gave his girls a hug and kiss, and then walked with Devon out to his Hummer.

"I'm going to have Brady stop by and check on you on his way down to San Diego. One of my old teammates is getting married, so I'm going to be holing up with Mark, but I'll be going to the wedding with everybody else. Brady said he would stop by and make sure everything was working, so be expecting that, okay?"

"I got it. No worries."

Nick had hired two retired Sonoma County Sheriff's deputies who were doing security guard work, plus a couple of Zak's buddies who could work in the fields as well as shoot straight. They agreed to put them up in the bunkhouse, which was an extension to the bottling center and the crush station. At first, Devon didn't want to have men she didn't know around her, but after she was introduced and learned what their backgrounds were, she relented.

The new men had started the day before yesterday, and Nicholas already knew they were the right choice.

"Now if you see or hear anything that you don't like, or you don't think you're protected somehow, you give me a call. I'm going to text you and call you every night, and I want to hear from you every day. I want to talk to the girls and make sure everything here is functioning like it should."

"Well, we don't have any events this week, just the normal tourist traffic. Are you sure we shouldn't just close down for a few days until you get back?"

Nick shook his head. "I don't want to look like we're doing anything different. I don't want him to think that we're getting prepared or that we're locking down and readying ourself for a war. I would rather he think we are clueless or oblivious to what he may have going on."

"What about the idea of trying to meet with him?"

"I'm going to talk about that, too, with the guys down there. I'll see if there's any interest in raising some money to try to buy the guy out. Maybe we can, I don't know. I know one person who isn't going to have any spare money, and that's Mark. He's already been complaining to me about his mortgage. But there are others down there, a couple lieutenant commanders and an admiral or two I can meet with. I thought the wedding would be a great time to make the rounds a little bit and get some information, see what people are into. I'll let you know. And trust me, Devon, I want the peaceful solution. That's what I want."

Devon hugged him tightly. "Promise me you'll come back safe and sound and ready for some romance. We spent so much time getting prepared, we kind of forgot about that part." She wrinkled up her nose for effect.

It melted Nick's heart. "I'm going to be thinking about nothing else all week, Sweetheart." He kissed her gently, dumped his bags in the second seat of his Hummer, waved, and took off down the gravel driveway, leaving a trail of dust behind him. At the gate, he used his clicker, which let him out. The camera flashed, taking a picture of him in the driver's seat, and he was pleased. Everything worked the way it was supposed to. The electrical wiring around the perimeter and the gates were in a failsafe mode. If the lines were cut, they would go into a backup battery pattern that could last for four days in a row. And if that failed, or if they had a power outage, they had installed an industrial-sized generator with enough power to run everything, even the bottling facility. That was something that had been super expensive to add, but Nicholas knew it was necessary.

He hoped he wasn't being too trusting of the systems and the men he'd asked to help him. But this was going to be the only way he could talk to his buddies and elicit the help he needed—at least without talking over the telephone or with a computer or with FaceTime. He needed to talk to them eyeball to eyeball. It was just the way they did things.

He drove straight through in one twelve-hour stretch, being careful not to speed except for places he knew he could get away with it. Approximately 8:00 at night, he knocked on Mark's front door.

Mark and Sophia had taken a little two-story ranch home about five blocks away from the beach. It was nearly a half a mile to the downtown strip, off the beaten path a bit but close to shopping, the kids' daycare, and Sophia's studio.

Mark answered the door with a beer. He was shirtless, barefoot, and wore brown flannel pajama bottoms. Pictures of bears decorated the fabric, and the sign *trophy husband* was plastered everywhere on his butt, his legs, and around the waistband.

Nick looked down at his drawstring pants and the beer and nodded. "Cool, so I can see you're really working up for that deployment, aren't you?"

"Get in here. We only have a few minutes to talk before Sophia comes home with the girls. I just want to hear it from you straight. You really think you're protected up there?"

"I've done everything I can, Mark. I want to try to see if there's some kind of a way we can resolve all of this, but I'm just... You know, at some point, they're all going to have to function to help themselves in their own protection. I've got Brady checking on them on the way down. He's coming for the wedding, you know?"

"Oh, cool, I haven't seen him in ages."

"And I've got a couple Sheriff's deputies that are on retirement who I can trust and some field workers that Zak knows. He's letting me borrow them for a while, people he trusts to put in charge of his vineyard when they're on vacation. So I think they're pretty good. So far, Devon likes them, the girls seem to be fine with it, and we've tried to make it a family experience. It's kind of crappy to have to go through all this, but you know, we got to do it."

"So what are you thinking regarding a peaceful solution then?"

"Well, like we said briefly, maybe get together a group to buy Rodriguez out? If he's willing?"

"You think he would?"

"I have no idea what his motivation is. If you wave enough money in front of people's eyes, they do unexpected things. You know, they say everything's available for a price."

"Not everything. Surely you don't mean *every-thing*?"

Nick realized he had misspoken. "No, not every-thing."

Mark walked into the kitchen and grabbed a cold beer out of the refrigerator for him and popped it open without asking him if he wanted one. Nick remembered that's the way Mark was.

"You going to show me around the place?" Nick asked.

"Okay, here's the kitchen. We got two bedrooms upstairs. We're downstairs, but the girls are upstairs. Come on. I'll show you."

Mark walked him through the whole house. The two girls shared the one bedroom upstairs for now but would eventually have their own room. Downstairs, in addition to the huge master with a crib already installed, was an office for Mark. Sophia also used it for doing her billing for her dance studio.

The home was minimally furnished, mostly done with shabby chic used pieces. Either donated or picked up at garage sales, Mark told him. But Nick thought it was attractive, uncluttered, and was a comfortable home. It was slightly smaller than Nick's, but it had a beautiful backyard with a swimming pool in it.

"This is nice, Mark. I bet the girls really love this pool. At least they will when they're older."

"Sophia has taught them both, even the baby. She floats like one of those blowup dolls we had. You remember that?"

"Mark, how could I forget?"

"They're the hit of the neighborhood, believe me. And Sophia has actually been giving swimming lessons to some of the other kids in the neighborhood too. Sort of little extra job with some side income. We're into water safety big time."

They sat down at a glass tabletop in the middle of the patio overlooking the pool. Nick remembered how balmy and even the San Diego weather was. There was a slight breeze, and even at 8:00 at night, it was warm, not like the tropics but warm. And they were close enough to the ocean where he could smell the salty air.

It was impossible to get away from the sounds of traffic in the area and of jets and airport noise, which was one big difference between being in San Diego and being up in Sonoma County. But he liked the weather, he liked the sunshine, and he liked the way it made him feel. He was relaxed, and it brought back happy memories of his training and years on the teams. They were some of the most important years of his life. Not necessarily his best years or his most pleasurable ones, but they were good years. That's where he learned to become a man.

"So who do you think I should talk to about this

investment thing if we can get a fund put together to offer to Rodriguez? Who do you think I should ask?"

Mark sighed and frowned a bit. "I think I'd first tell Kyle. He doesn't like you or anybody talking to his guys without him knowing about it. You know how he is about that."

"Oh, yeah. Gee, I talked to him—what was it?—two weeks ago when he was up at Joshua's wedding."

"Oh, that's right. I forgot you guys talked. But you didn't know anything about Rodriguez then, is that right?"

"Yep, didn't have a clue."

"Well, then I think I'd go talk to Libby's dad. I don't know if you know, but her mother passed away."

"I heard that. That's a shame. She was a nice lady."

"Well, he's kind of got a new girlfriend, if you could believe it, and it turns out, she was someone who was actually involved with his twin brother at the time he was killed in Grenada."

"No shit?"

"Yeah, it was a little strange for Libby. She wasn't quite sure she trusted her, but she's got a cousin who is very athletic. I mean, the two of them look like twins practically. And they've been pretty close friends. The mother, Melissa, moved to Coronado earlier this year. I think it's a good thing."

"So Dr. Brownlee, he has a live-in then?" Nick

wanted to know.

"Not quite, but I think they're getting ready. We'll see. You'll get to see him at the wedding. I'm sure he'll be there."

Libby was married to Calvin Cooper, one of their medics on SEAL Team 3, and Dr. Brownlee, who was a noted psychiatrist, frequent talk show host, and interviewed nationwide, was an expert on PTSD and had worked with many of the SEALs on SEAL Team 3 and other teams as well. He had been an advisor to just about anybody that Nicholas knew who had a problem coming back from a bad deployment. In addition to investing in Sophie's Choice, he also was an investor in Zak and Amy's winery, going back some almost ten years now.

"Okay, who else, anybody else?"

"Well, I'm not exactly a magnet for people with money. People with money tend to avoid me, because it seems like I need money all the time. We run out of it constantly. I can't save a thing. And if it wasn't for Sophia and her dance studio and her lessons on the side and anything else she can get, I honestly don't know if we could keep this house. We really need a bigger house with the baby coming, and we can't do it. Besides my credit's kind of crappy. I don't think I could qualify for a loan."

"Mark, as long as your family's healthy, as long as

you're all living together and you're able to make ends meet, just call it a day. Call it done and good, okay?"

Nick was beginning to see some signs of perhaps worry and depression on his old friend. It bothered him.

"Yeah, but do I have to re-up again? I've got like two years, maybe a year and a half to go. If I get that bonus again, it'll probably pay off everything we have, except the mortgage. It's just that... Shit, Nick, I never wanted to be a twenty-year man. I was a one and done, or maybe two, you know. Then when I got hooked up with Sophia, well, she wanted a house, and I wanted to give her that house. And I had never been a saver before, so I've kind of been stuck into this whole business of re-upping. And that's what it's looking like again. Because I don't know where I could get my hands on that kind of money. We need to get our debts paid off."

Nick was uncomfortable talking about financial matters with Mark. He felt it was none of his business, and he was a little ashamed he was seeing an unresponsible slice of who Mark was.

"Why don't you open up a security company, your own private security? You could do that."

"I don't think so. I'm just not good at business. I'm not good at buying cars. I'm not good at investing in anything. I even tried to go into some crypto, and God,

I lost my shirt. I just bought it the wrong time."

"But no gambling. Right?"

Mark shook his head vehemently. "Other than the crypto, and that was a hell of a gamble, nope, no gambling. I keep the drinking down a little bit, and I just devote all my time when I'm home to training and helping Sophia and the girls. It's going to get easier, but with them both being so little, she's really got her hands full, and she's tired all the time. I can't let her be that way. It's hard enough when I go."

Nick wasn't sure what to say.

"Don't mind me. We'll figure it out."

Nicholas knew he would have to speak to Devon first, but he posed something he hoped Mark might appreciate. "What if you took a leave of absence after this next deployment or ask for a leave of absence to come up and help me? I could put you on the payroll. If you wanted to bring the kids, you could, but you might not want to do that because of our potential neighbor returning. We've got great hospitals in case Sophia wanted to stay up there, but I could use the help. And I could pay you for it."

"Can't leave her and the girls alone."

"Can they stay with someone else? With another family? Or do you have a relative who could come, give her a hand?"

"She's close with another dancer who trains at the

studio and teaches her classes when she has to skip. I guess we could ask her. Sophia would probably prefer living with her than with me, at the present time."

"You gotta fix that, Mark. Not wise, if that's happening."

"You're right, of course. Her family is all in Italy. Maybe her mother could come over. That would be fun for her. At least I think it would be. But I'll check with her tonight."

"I pose it because we've done well. And Devon still dabbles in some real estate. We've managed some good savings. We just don't have enough to buy the property next door. Mark, maybe it would be something you need. Maybe you just need a break, and then you could come back to all this and resume your life. What do you think?"

Mark studied his face carefully before he answered. "That's an idea, Nicholas. I would love to come back up there and spend some time. And if you could use me and pay me, well, if Kyle lets me off, that might not be a bad idea."

CHAPTER 6

TREVOR AND BAILEY'S wedding was a lavish affair, held in the old Presbyterian church, and although they didn't create a destination wedding, they spent a fortune transforming the church sanctuary and fellowship hall into a beautiful bucolic oasis of flowers. Nick had never seen so many flower bouquets, even one hanging upside down centered in the middle of the dance floor at the reception.

One of the nice things about the San Diego area in early summer was that anywhere you went you heard the chirping of birds. Several of Nick's friends who had traveled to Florida and other places south had remarked that the same thing occurred in the tropics.

He, Mark, and family arrived early, and he was given the youngest of the two girls, Ophelia, to carry around the courtyard outside and otherwise preoccupy, while her older sister, Carrie Anne, was getting her diaper changed. Ophelia was just barely walking, all decked out in her pale yellow outfit, including lace booties and a bonnet. However, Carrie Anne walked much later and was not as tall, so most people thought the two were twins.

Nick had always enjoyed the baby stages of his girls, so he patiently showed her flowers, butterflies, and leaves that rustled in the gentle breeze of the early afternoon San Diego environs.

"See all these pretty flowers, Ophelia?" he asked as he took the youngster closer to the row of urns filled with white lilies, baby's breath, tuberoses, and plumeria blossoms.

Bailey's father was from San Diego, a Navy man, but her mother was of Hawaiian descent. Therefore, the entire wedding party was decked out in flower leis, which created a sumptuous and head-spinning aroma. It reminded Nick of the way Hawaii had smelled when he stepped off the plane. He swore last time he visited there that he could smell the flowers, the ocean, and even the clouds above.

Ophelia tried to reach out and touch several of the leis on some of the wedding party and loved the large showy displays at the front of the church, but Nick was quick to make sure she didn't grab anything to pull it over. He didn't want to cause a scene that might ruin Bailey's day.

"There she is, my little princess," Mark said. "You

do that quite well, Nick," Mark added, taking Ophelia from his arms.

"She's a real beauty. Very curious. I remember those days, just seems like yesterday, doesn't it?"

"That it does." Mark bounced Ophelia around and pointed to a bird that had landed in the ivy vines growing up the side of the old church, and shortly after it disappeared into the white and gray-green leaves, they heard the unmistakable chirping of baby birds.

Ophelia's eyes widened, and then she giggled.

"Dinner delivered," said Nick.

Several of the SEALs had worn their uniforms, but not all of them. Nick had brought a jacket and wore it with jeans and a light-colored yellow shirt. He would have been the only man under forty who would wear a tie if he had brought one. He left the shirt collar open. Several wives, dates, and girlfriends, mostly women he didn't recognize, were decked out to the nines, fluttering around the garden area and back of the church, waiting for a place to light.

As the pews began to fill up, Nick took a place toward the rear instead of joining Mark and his family, who sat up in the second row. Mark wore his dress whites.

The music began, and Trevor nervously walked with his mother down the aisle, depositing her on the side, next to other family members. He stayed up near the altar and waited for the sight of his bride to appear.

Nick studied the backs of several uniformed service members, several silver-haired gentlemen, and lots of young men and women in their twenties and thirties. There were very few children, but those who did attend were dressed in their Sunday best. Several of the wives he recognized were now pregnant, towing toddlers, or carrying babies. The men hugged and shook hands, and he was sure that sitting in the back, away from all the scrutiny, was where he felt the most comfortable.

All of a sudden, Brady deposited his gnarly frame next to Nick.

"There you are, Sport," Brady whispered in his raspy voice.

Nick smelled alcohol and garlic fries on his breath and knew perhaps he'd met with the groomsmen earlier and had been involved in a toast or two, but he wasn't drunk. He'd just been drinking alcohol.

Brady leaned into him, their shoulders touching, and whispered, "Stopped by and checked on Devon. She probably told you."

"She did," Nick answered. "Thanks for doing that. Everything look okay?"

"From what I can tell, yes. You got some good guys working there, Nick. They're hard workers. They didn't want me to get anywhere near her until I explained who I was. That was a good sign. I didn't give them hell for it either. They were just doing their job."

"Good to hear. How's your family?"

"We're doing amazingly well. I'm hoping for no drama for the next twelve months." He turned and angled his head so Nick would look at him straight in the eyes. "You think I can manage that?" He squinted as he said this.

"Beats me, Brady. Just when I think things have calmed down, they all go to shit again."

Apparently, he had spoken a little too loudly, because a silver-haired woman turned around and scowled at him, putting her forefinger to her lips.

Brady shrugged. "Well, you can't please all the people all the time, can you?"

"Ain't that the truth?"

The organ music morphed into a processional march as one by one the bridesmaids made their gorgeous entrance. Nick thought to himself that Devon would have loved seeing this spectacle. She always liked showy events, special celebrations. Of course, that's what they were in the business to do in Sonoma County. But she would have loved the way the church looked in colors of white, light pink, and pale yellow while the men dressed in their dress whites or white tuxes. It was quite the beautiful sight.

"Do you suppose they'll mind if I take a picture with no flash?" Nick asked Brady. "I know Devon would love to see this."

"Just take it," said Brady. "Always better to ask for forgiveness than permission."

That was one hundred percent right.

Nick got his cell phone out and was able to get a shot of Trevor's nervous face, his uniformed best man standing next to him, and the lovely ladies on the opposite side. He took a picture of Brady's face, which, at less than 12 inches, morphed into something that reminded him more of an ogre movie than the face of one of the best and most dependable SEAL team members he'd ever met. Brady was as true with his word as any man ever was. He had left the teams shortly before Nick did, and everyone missed him.

At last, the church was instructed to stand as Bailey and her father made their way down the center aisle. She did look like a Cinderella princess right out of Disneyland, twinkling with crystals everywhere, her auburn hair in ringlets piled on top her head and cascading down the back of her neck and over her beautiful smooth shoulders. Her Hawaiian heritage from her mother's side gave her complexion a light tan coffee color. And it was stunning in contrast to the white gown and veil and crystals. Trevor's eyes were fixated on Bailey as she whispered to her father and he returned the conversation, until they were at last at the bottom step of the altar.

This wedding was a little respite for Nick, somebody's perfect moment, a nice sunshiny day, nobody dying or crying out, nobody bloodied or wounded, and no explosions. It was just an island of peace, a celebration, in the middle of an uncertain world.

Just as he had done at home, Nick decided that he would cherish, absorb, and bring home to Devon all the joy and beauty of this day.

THE RECEPTION WAS held in the nearby fellowship hall, which probably indicated that Bailey's parents were church members since the outside public wasn't allowed use of it. While Bailey's parents may have saved in day rental fees, they completely went over the top with the food, the wine, and the music. There was a jazz combo playing in the background and a full four-course sit-down dinner served by waiters in tuxes and white gloves.

Next to him, Brady was bemoaning the fact that he knew he was going to spill on his shirt and that Maggie would get after him for it.

"That's what the shirt's for, to protect your skin from all that stuff you're about to put in your mouth. Right, Brady?"

"It's never easy when I go to these things. I feel like I'm going to break everything I touch. It's just not my way of doing things. But I'm here to celebrate their day, and I have to talk to Kyle."

"What's up, Brady, if I may ask?"

"Ah, it's not much. But I wanted to ask his opinion about something. I've been doing some little side work, nothing too heavy, security, light bodyguard duty, and I found it pays well. They're asking me to do other things, and really, I had intended to just stay home and work on the farm. This guy I don't know called me up and offered me some serious cash to do work for his group. Maybe you know who he is, Riley-something?"

"Colin Riley, the guy in the wheelchair?"

"Yeah, that's him. I just wanted to know what Kyle thought of him. Like, is he trustworthy."

"You're not actually considering going to work for the guy, are you?"

"Just because I was asked to accompany some senators on a fact-finding mission down in Mexico. It's not an op at all. It's just to accompany them, and perhaps tell them a little bit about what we went through. But it's through Riley's company. He runs private security for a lot of people in Washington."

"I've heard that. I wouldn't do it if I were you. It's too unpredictable there." Nick saw an opportunity he decided to exploit. After he pointed out the small piece of lettuce and salad dressing stuck to the front of Brady's shirt, he proposed a question. "If you're looking for work… you know about my neighbor, and you know I've hired some people to help keep Devon and the girls safe. I'm just using people I know and trust. If it's extra money you're looking for—"

"No, I'm set there. I don't really have to do it. But hell, Nick, for you, I'll do whatever I can. But no, I'm not interested in a job. I just, well, I was going to turn it down, and Maggie said I should maybe check with Kyle since I was coming here anyway. We've both made a vow to each other that we're not going to do any more ops, and this would not be it. But honestly, the security, the Secret Service, that those guys have, they're making walking targets out of those people. They're not safe at all."

"I know it. We've all seen that. Who could forget the ambassador in the Canary Islands, right?"

"Well, that was after my time. That's when Zak got injured, right?" Brady asked.

"Yes, sir. But seriously, Brady, if you want to do some good for some people, forget the congressmen and the senators and the vice president. Stick with regular folks. Regular folks are the ones who need it the most. Those guys can hire whomever they want. They can drive down there in a bullet-proof personnel carrier. I'm the one who needs help. So consider it, okay?" Nick asked him.

Brady nodded and stared down at his half-eaten dinner then pushed it with the palm of his right hand into the center of the table. He looked like something in the conversation upset his stomach.

"So you're here to ask for assistance, I'm guessing?" he asked Nick.

"Yep. I also need to talk to several of the others. Trying to come up with some kind of a way that we can maybe buy my neighbor out."

"Well, that would solve a lot, wouldn't it?"

"Sure would."

"So how much do you need?" Brady asked.

"I'm thinking he's probably going to want five or six million dollars for that property. It's not worth that, but it would be if it had water to it. I just don't know if he wants the money or not, and so I thought I'd see what I could roust up down here."

"That's a hell of an idea. It would be nice if he'd take the money and run. From all the comments I've heard others make, that guy is just rotten to the core. And your story about how he got out, boy, I don't know what I'd do. But I do know a couple of ways to solve the problem permanently. You know, Nicholas, you can count on me if that's what you want done."

Nick realized this was the second time in less than a week that somebody had offered to assassinate his enemy. He wondered how many more times before the end of the day he would hear the same thing again.

As the dancing began and the bride and groom

sashayed across the dance floor, SEALs and their wives and girlfriends stood talking in groups, some all men, some mixed men and women. Whenever the children got together, they always seemed to form a rat pack of unruly young citizens, dancing in groups of four or five, running when they shouldn't, and occasionally tripping. A couple of the older boys, including Kyle's son Brandon, got into the champagne.

Nick wondered whether he should seek out Kyle and let him know and decided that was probably somebody else's job. But he did keep an eye on the young boy, who was growing up to be the spitting image of his father, very athletic of course, and probably headed to follow in his father's footsteps as a SEAL someday. It wasn't uncommon for that to happen in their community.

At last, he spotted Kyle and made his way across the room to speak to him.

"Nice to see you again so soon, Kyle."

"Hey there! Now where is Christy?" He searched the room, finally locating her. "She made me promise we wouldn't leave until she got to say hello. You have a real fan there. Am I missing something?" Kyle asked.

Again, this was the second time in a week somebody had made some kind of reference to another SEAL wife and teased of a relationship that didn't exist.

"I will make sure that I see her."

Kyle introduced Nick to several young SEAL candidates who had been trained by various men in Kyle's unit. These were fresh-faced, barely old enough to shave, and looked like junior high schoolers, although they were probably all in their twenties. Their cheeks were rosy, baby-faced, and they had that look in their eyes announcing they were ready for action but a little bit afraid they weren't up to the task. He nodded as he shook hands with all of them.

"You stick close to this guy. He won't steer you wrong. If you make a team and you get a request in for a west coast team, make sure you get on Kyle's. I think there are a lot of men today who are alive because of this gentleman right here. He runs a tight ship, but man, some of the things we've gotten into." He started to shake his head and looked at Kyle, who began to laugh.

"Well, let's not get into all those things. Suffice it to say we have a good time, we play hard, and we party hard too," said Kyle.

"I'm going to steal him away from you guys for just a few minutes," said Nick. "I promise to bring him right back."

He pulled Kyle to the side by placing the palm of his right hand at the top of Kyle's spine and leaned in to whisper in his ear. "I got bad news, Kyle."

Kyle's back became rigid. He stiffly mumbled,

"Okay. Let's hear it."

"Enemario Rodriguez has been released from prison."

Nick stepped back, because that's all he had to say, and when Kyle reacted, he could see the alert and the concern in his eyes. His jaw was clenched.

"You got to be kidding me, Nick. How could that happen?"

"He got off on a technicality, one of those projects that goes back and reviews charging documents, making sure there were no procedural errors created. I don't understand all of it, and I don't want to, and if I look into it, I'll get really pissed, Kyle. But I'm in a little bit of a pickle. I have to protect Devon and the girls. I don't know what this guy's going to do."

"Have you told anybody else?" Kyle asked.

"Well, Brady knows, because I asked him to check on Devon and the girls on his way down here. Of course, Zak knows. I've talked to Mark, as well. But that's it."

"Okay, so I give it two, three days, and then the entire team will know. You know that's going to happen, Nick. You guys are worse than a stitch and bitch session."

"I do."

"So how are we going to play this?"

Nick liked the fact that Kyle said *we* and not *you.*

"I came to get advice. Mark is considering asking you for some time off, to come up and give me a hand."

Kyle's beady eyes seared him all the way through. "Help you as in what, exactly?" His face was alert, his emotions dangling on the edge of a cliff. Nick knew exactly what was going through Kyle's mind.

"Just protection, Kyle. But I have some options. None of them include getting rid of the enemy. I'm not going there. I want a peaceful solution to this. But as you know, evil people do all sorts of evil things. And I've got to protect my girls, or I have to sell and move. I'll do anything to keep them safe, and I don't want to do anything illegal, but I feel like I need help. And I need some good honest advice. Do you suppose tomorrow or the next day I could sit down with you, and we could talk?"

"Yes. Yes, let's do that. Do you mind if I bring Cooper and a few other people over?"

"No, the more the better. Like I said, I'm looking for ideas. Mark said he'd ask you for a leave. It's your choice whether you want to divulge I've told you that, but I promise to keep him out of trouble if I can."

"Oh shit, keeping Mark out of trouble? Don't promise something you can't do, Nick. I'm not the problem there. He's got a few marks on his record. He's getting a little strong and testy lately. I think maybe staying up half the night and changing diapers and having another one on the way has him at wit's end, and you know how Mark is. He's stressing. He doesn't comprehend it's a good kind of stress, and it'll never be over. But he's stressing. I personally think the break would be good for him. But some of the others are asking me if I should recommend he be removed from the team or placed in some administrative capacity. Perhaps take a rotation or two, language school or some other program or a BUDS instructor for half a year. He needs a break. He's got a lot on his mind. And I'm not sure things are happy at home. You need to know that, Nick."

Nick appreciated the honesty Kyle showed him.

"Okay, I walk in with my eyes open. I'm here to listen, to learn, to get ideas. I've secured the house, electrified our perimeter fencing, and installed cameras. I've taken Devon shooting, and I've done some self-defense work with the girls. We're addressing this head-on. There's also one other option."

"What option?" Kyle asked.

"We can try to buy him out. And I have no idea whether he'd do that."

"Okay, so that's a possibility."

"I need some people who might be interested. Zak thought perhaps Libby's dad might. Besides that, I really don't know who to ask.

"How much did you say? Five million?"

"Five or six. Devon seems to think that's fair market value if it had water, and it doesn't. It needs my water to make it profitable. So the land is or could be valuable to me, but without water, it's useless to anybody else. Which is how all this happened in the first place."

Kyle was nodding his head, one arm crossed his chest, the other hand up to his mouth, his forefinger tapping against his lip. "So we'll explore that too. How about we meet tomorrow at nine o'clock at the Scupper?"

"Good for me. I'm all ears."

"I'm going to ask you if you really think Mark is the right person to help you. I mean he might be a little distracted, Nick."

"I don't think so, Kyle. I think it's going to be a return to a happier time in his life. A more carefree time. There's a part of Mark, I think, who would always be in love with Sophie even though she's no longer here with us. And in his mind, Mark is still defending her. He didn't even flinch when I asked him to come up and help me."

"Son, you've gotten very wise in your old age. I think you hit it right on the head. He couldn't save her, but he could help her brother. That's got to stay just between the two of us."

"Agreed. And it especially must be kept from Sophia," Nick murmured.

CHAPTER 7

NICK HAD A rather fitful night sleeping on the couch in Mark and Sophia's living room. Their little Cockapoo jumped up on his chest several times, scaring the crap out of him. In addition, Otis liked to lick Nick's face, which was extremely offensive to him. He liked dogs, but he didn't like little smelly dogs.

Otis was both of those.

Stumbling out of bed early, Nick changed into some running shorts, and decided to take a ten-mile run before the rest of the house got up. He didn't mind the baby crying in the middle of the night or the pattering around in the kitchen that was done. He'd been through those experiences years ago, and actually, they brought back fond memories.

But Otis was a deal breaker. In fact, Nick was going to tell Mark that he was going to hit a local motel instead of staying there one more night, unless he could conjure up an invite somewhere else.

He made it down to the beach very quickly, inhaling the misty salt air as the sun was beginning to rise in the east. It turned clouds out in the bay a bright pink, then rose, and everything became a light gray as the colors faded in the sunshine. The sky turned bright blue, and the sun domineered the whole region. It made the bay and ocean beyond appear it was made of liquid silver.

He wound up going back and forth the same stretch of beach three times before moving inland. Weaving through the neighborhoods doing five or six blocks at a time, he occasionally hit a dead-end road and had to double back and find another route from the beach. He tried to avoid traffic as much as possible, and as the sleepy little Coronado community began to wake up, he smelled bacon and coffee. He heard little snippets of conversations, ordinary life just drifting by as he ran.

It felt good to be by himself, where he could think. It also felt good to have the support of the man he was going to meet with this morning at the Scupper. Mark had been in a rather strange mood last night, and Nick overheard an argument between him and Sophia, which concerned him. Now he could see some of the thoughts Kyle had warned him about.

He pressed all that to the edges of his mind, focused home—on the beautiful valley of the moon, the way the fresh white linen moon shone magically, pouring itself into the valley floor, affecting the tides, the animals as they scurried about in the evening, and the way it pulled at humans and their frail hearts.

He imagined the faces of his beautiful daughters, sleeping. He saw Devon tucked safely in their bed, having brought little Sophia in with her. He couldn't wait to get back there.

Patience. Soon, Nick. Time to gather information for the operation that was so critical to the health and safety of your family, he told himself.

He made his way back to Mark's house, after getting lost for the last fifteen minutes of his run. He finally saw the black iron fencing and gate, looking quite New Orleans-style, with a meandering brick path up to the red front door. It was a beautiful Dutch colonial style home, the second story having been added twenty or thirty years prior, when the owner had installed flawless white oak flooring throughout the whole house, even the kitchen. Even with the addition and other remodeling, the previous owners still kept the pitch of the roof and the small panes on the windows. Painted light grey with cream trim made the red door a focal point. It was a cheerful, happy home.

Even though last night it wasn't.

Inside the front door, Nick could hear the chaos of this Navy SEAL family's day beginning.

He double-checked with Mark before he jumped into the bathroom of the hallway. He didn't want to be the one tying up a shower when someone else needed it.

Refreshed and cleaned, feeling good from his run, he walked barefoot into the kitchen to see if he could find the coffee that he smelled.

Sophia was scrambling some eggs, making an omelet with vegetables from her backyard.

"My favorite. We do this all the time at our place," said Nick, admiring the cheesy dish.

Sophia turned to him, still in her nightie. Her belly looked like it had expanded at least two inches since the day before. He couldn't help but stare down at her, the evidence of her belly button turning inside out, protruding like a small child's thumb from under her pink gown. Noting the trajectory of his gaze, she drew the robe closer up over her shoulders and tied the ribbon under her chin to protect a view of her chest.

She was a stunningly beautiful woman, and her body still moved as a graceful dancer, though her center of gravity had been altered with the impending birth. Her fiery Italian anger and feisty attitude, so often expressed in her dance moves, even when she was teaching ballroom, were a challenge for Mark, Nick remembered.

But Nick felt accepted.

"It's just about the only thing I can keep down these days. I thought the morning sickness would go away once I hit six months, but I think I'm going to be sick all the way through," she said in her lilting Italian accent, as graceful as her movements.

She looked down, placed her hand over the bulge, and smiled. Nick knew that look, that of a woman waiting for something miraculous to occur. He felt the need to tell her.

"Well, you look beautiful, Sophia. Pregnancy agrees with you. I remember Devon's cheeks were so pink. I honestly think a woman is the prettiest when she's pregnant. It's not a wives' tale. It's the truth." He smiled which she eagerly returned.

"So you perhaps have some work for Mark. Is that what's going on?"

She was always direct, laser-focused on giving direction or expressing something.

"Well, I suppose it's up to Kyle, but he seemed to be into it. Maybe it would do Mark some good to come up North to get away."

"Get away, or run away?" she asked, still examining his face.

"He'd never run away. That part of Mark won't ever change, no matter how old she is. My personal opinion is that it's never a good idea to go on a deployment when you're worried or stressed. He wants to be there for the baby, Sophia, and you know he's concerned about the money."

"He told you all that?"

"Hoping I'm not getting him into trouble, but yes, he did."

"But I'm the one having the baby, watching Ophelia and Carrie Anne when he's gone."

"He wouldn't be granted leave under other circumstances. You know we miss births all the time. This way, he'll be home sooner, safe and sound. Ready to be your house slave so you can enjoy your new little one. But hey, I'm a man, and what do I know? I just need someone like Mark to help me out. And I thought it would be doing him, and you, a favor."

She separated the egg mixture onto three large plates and one little one. After adding some fruit, she tossed everything into the sink, washed her hands, and shoved his plate into his chest.

"Eat."

Nick was concerned she didn't approve of the plan.

"Do you have someone you can bring to the house to help you with the kids, or do you have some relatives nearby you could visit, perhaps stay with?"

"I'd probably be okay by myself, but yes, a couple of the wives are going take turns staying with me. The ladies without family yet will be missing their husbands on deployment, so it all works out. You know that. We take care of our own. I've done the same for others. I always have help with babysitting, as long as I reciprocate."

Nick knew this all to be true. That part of the Brotherhood he missed.

"That's the nice thing about the teams," she added, setting her dish on the table. "Everyone works together to make it work."

"How are your parents in Italy?" Nick asked.

"Oh my mother, I miss her. I am not sure when I'll be able to go back there to visit. She has no money for a visit here, and she's not in the best of health. But my brother and his wife look after her. We FaceTime with the girls, and she loves it."

"That's nice. I'm afraid my kids lost out on my end. Both my parents are gone. So you're lucky, even though they only get to see her on FaceTime."

"So how long do you think Mark will be there?"

"I'm guessing it'll be two to three weeks. At least enough time to get us over the hurdle, while we figure out what our neighbor's intentions are. Until then, we're going to try to live our lives as we were before. Just be extra vigilant."

They could hear the squeal of little girl laughter as Mark was getting his young soldiers dressed after a bath and having a time of it.

Nick chuckled. "He's pretty handy. I gotta hand it

to him."

"Oh, he is that. Who knew?"

She gave Nick a respectful smile, but he could see there was some pain there under the laugh lines at the sides of her lips.

"I really appreciate Mark's help, and I suspect when he comes back home, he's going to want to grow some grapes in your backyard. I promised to help him catch the fever."

She laughed at that. "It would be nice to see Mark have something he catches fire about. I often wonder if we didn't jump into all this too soon, and now with a third child on the way, we just really didn't have enough time to ourselves first. If I were to do it over, I would give us more time together."

"Well, you can always look at it this way, your girls will be off at college or working somewhere in the world, and you and Mark will have that alone time a little earlier than some parents do. Maybe that's the best way to look at it."

She went back to stirring the eggs on her plate, hesitating to finish them. She stabbed a piece of bell pepper and a cherry tomato from the mixture and swallowed it down.

"From your garden?" Nick asked, showing the pepper on his fork.

"Yessir. Healthy, good exercise. Hoping the girls

take to it when they get older."

"You like the gardening, Sophia?"

"I like planting, but I don't like weeding. The weeding part, that's not for me. And now with the pregnancy, it's nearly impossible for me to do that and remain comfortable. But I love to plant things and see how well they'll grow. And we can grow so many things here. Like back home in Italy, along the Mediterranean coast. They used to say you put a stick in the ground and it would grow. The soil was heavy volcanic, but it was great for tomatoes and growing huge melons." She was staring out the window when she added, "Grapes, of course, as well."

"I think Italy is one of the prettiest countries I've ever visited. My favorite was Capri."

"Ah, Capri! Honeymooners' paradise. Pink Bougainvillea flowers over cobblestone fences and sides of buildings. So quaint with the blue Mediterranean in the distance. Yes, now you're making me homesick."

"I'm sorry, Sophia. That was unthinking of me." Mark entered the dining area, examining the plates while holding the squirming Ophelia in his arms and helping Carrie Anne climb into her highchair.

"So we got two freshly dressed kids, straight from the tub. I'm not sure they'll eat eggs this morning, sweetheart," he said to Sophia as he pulled the second highchair up to the table and deposited his chubby youngest girl in it. She slapped the white plastic tray and babbled something in Italian, which Sophia answered.

"They're learning languages already," Nick remarked.

"Best way to learn."

"I'm even learning as they do," added Mark. "What do we do if they don't eat the eggs?"

"That's okay. I have cereals in the cabinet. Let Carrie Anne pick."

They all sat together as a family, the girls both in high chairs even though their three-year-old could sit in a regular chair. The baby took a frozen pancake they'd cooked for her and shredded it into tiny pieces all over the tray. Then with one quick flick of the arm, she scraped the entire contents, butter, syrup, and all, onto the ground, flying in all directions.

"Oops," Mark said, his fork midway to his mouth.

Sophia leaned into her hand, her elbow at the table, closing her eyes. She let her fingers massage her temples. "Oh my God. I just don't have the energy to pick that up today."

"Not to worry," said Nick. "I'm at your service, madame."

Nick pulled some paper towels from the kitchen, wadded up all the mess from the floor, twisted the paper towels together to secure the crumbs, and dropped it in the garbage can. Then he put soap on the sponge and brought it over to clean out the hardwood floors so they didn't have a sticky residue left behind.

He checked his watch and announced he was going to head out to the Scupper.

"But you've already eaten, Nick," said Sophia.

"It's a meeting. It's just a get together with the guys. Mark, are you able to come?"

Mark scowled and then asked Sophia if she needed him for anything over the next hour or two, and she agreed it was okay, thanking him for getting the girls up and dressed. "If you could, try to be back before lunchtime."

"Roger that, sweetheart," Mark said as he kissed her on the cheek.

The two of them rode down the strand until the familiar wooden doors of the Scupper showed up. Mark was able to get a parking space right in front, something he used to boast about doing all the time when they were on the teams together.

"Kyle said he's going to bring along a couple other people. Hopefully, it's not a crowd," said Nick.

"No, that's how he does it. He brings several people in so everyone can speak freely, and he gets everybody's opinion, and then he makes his decision. In this case, it's *your* decision, but Kyle works only one way."

"You know, one of the things I didn't mention to

you before is we might be able to help you out, Mark, if you find yourself in a situation where you can't function or make your payments. I talked to Devon last night, and she's agreed that, up to a certain point, we could try to help you if you need it. I think we'd prefer you pay off your debts first before you go buying a bigger house. So that's kind of our rules, but you figure out what it would take for you to get debt-free, except for the mortgage, and maybe we can do that."

Mark didn't react to the offer.

Nick continued, "You'll be making a salary, of course, as we discussed, but we might be able to lend you or perhaps gift you some small amount beyond that. I just want you to know. Please ask me if you need something."

Mark remained silent, which was a bit awkward. The car had stopped, and the two of them sat there, not getting out to join the others. Nick wanted to wait for Mark to find the words he was searching for.

"I really appreciate you, Nick. But I don't want to be a burden to anybody. I also have a rule not to borrow from another team guy. I think we'll be fine. The little extra working for you for a few weeks, that will help. But I thank you for the offer, and I'm going to trust that we'll be able to work things out. I can always do an early enlistment on our next deployment. That would give us some cash ahead of time. I'm just not a hundred percent sold on the idea yet."

"My solution, Mark, is to think about it then talk it over and over again. List the pros and cons and really do a thorough search of yourself, your needs, where that will put you, and what's the best for your family before you make that final decision. You and I both know being a SEAL is dangerous stuff. You have to ask yourself is it going to be any easier on Sophia if something happens to you while you're on deployment? You know it can always happen. With your kids so little, maybe the writing's on the wall for that. But I don't want to tell you what to do or suggest what you need to do. You do what's good for you guys. I will gratefully accept whatever help you can give us."

Before they got out of the car, Mark punched Nick in the arm, and it hurt.

"Thanks, man. And yeah, I know you'll get me back."

Walking into the dark interior of the Scupper brought him back, the team hangout with pictures of flags and stations where the team posed in front of a building of some kind or a country flag somewhere. Some of the teams, especially the older ones, made campaign flags. Several from the Vietnam era graced the walls of the Scupper, along with pictures of heroes long retired or gone, bad guys who had been eliminated from the face of the earth, and all things in between.

There were photos of blown-up Humvees, crash landings, halo jumps, and some of the skydiving antics they liked to do on the weekends. Some from the legendary bonfires graced the walls, where the whole team would get together on the beach before they deployed, including the wives and the kids. There were pictures of three sets of twins by guys on SEAL team five, all born the same day. And, of course, there were also photos of some of the men who didn't make it home, surrounded and supported by pictures of happy memories all around them.

Nothing is ever forgotten. We don't leave them behind, ever, Nick thought. It brought tears to his eyes, and he was grateful for the darkness, which masked them.

It felt like stepping back in time. He was twenty-one-years-old again, full of himself. His most favorite pastime on the weekends was going to a karaoke bar, drinking way too much, and singing off-key. He liked to belt out all the Elvis songs and worked on trying to get some of the hip movements in there as well. But those were the days when everything was an adventure, long before he had the obligations, long before he knew about his sister's illness and then her eventual death, before Devon came and saved him in every way possible.

He saw the group of men in the back room, all

lined up on both sides of a long wood plank table. A couple of the guys he had not seen before. Two of them had beers in front of them. Most everyone had eggs, biscuits, orange juice, and coffee. It all smelled and looked good, but Nick didn't have room.

Kyle stood up, crossed the floor in three long strides, and shook his hand again. "Nice to see you, Son."

Nick always thought it was funny how Kyle called them all 'son.' Though he was generally older than the rest of them, he only preceded them in age by less than ten years. By no means was Kyle considered the old man. There were several on the team who were way past forty.

But Kyle was the force of the team, the decision maker, the glue, the conscience of the group, the liaison between them and the head shed, the one who strategized and planned their ops, often with help from other agencies. Kyle kept them safe, helped remind them they were part of a Brotherhood, not just a job or a team. That not only they were on the team but their wives and children were part of the same Brotherhood. Reminding everybody that no one was ever left behind. Never to give up on any of them. Once a member of Seal Team 3, always and forever a member.

Regardless of the outcome.

It wasn't that Nick had forgotten about all of that.

In fact, he was hoping that's exactly what he'd find today. He was suddenly concerned about getting them too involved.

"Okay, so you know Fredo here, and you know Coop."

Both Coop and Fredo waived to Nick.

"You know TJ, but we've got several others here I'm not sure if you know. Rory?" Kyle asked.

"Nope. I think he's after my time."

"And we've got a couple who might come straggling in. I decided to include as many as could come, only because I wanted them all to hear it from you. All of the guys who helped that day at your sister's place, they were all asked to attend, but not everybody could with so little notice."

"Thanks, everybody." Nick remained standing while Kyle took his seat at the end of the table on the left side.

From his seated position, Kyle barked up at him, "So will you please tell the group about Rodriguez and why we should care. I mean all of you know we do care, but I want you to give them the why."

"Will do."

Nick stared down at the dirty plates, reached forward, grabbed a cup of coffee, and gulped half of it down. He was still collecting his thoughts when Jameson Daniels walked in, slapped him on the back, and gave him a wry smile.

"I can't believe you're here," Nick exclaimed. "I thought, well, I don't know what I thought. So you're still with this team. Kyle, you haven't kicked him off yet?" Nick asked.

Jameson and his wife had been married at the winery at Nick's. It was one of the first SEAL weddings they had there after they inherited and renovated the property with some of Sophie's insurance proceeds.

"I wouldn't miss it for all the tea in China," Jameson said. "And my wife sends her regards," he added, pretending to tip his imaginary cowboy hat.

While Jameson took a seat, Nick began the explanation. It was just like any other mission, where he needed to tell them what it was he needed and make the offer, the pitch for help.

He described what he'd done so far to protect the family, he described some of the personnel he'd added, and he also indicated he was constantly getting updated as far as what was going on with the adjacent property.

"I got state of the art surveillance. It sends me photo updates every night. Got a generator, too, so we won't miss a beat if we get bad weather or someone tries to cut us off, which is more likely."

The crowd nodded, listened, and paid attention to every word he said.

"One thing I want to try first is to try to negotiate with him. That means we've got to raise some money, and I don't want you to say anything in front of the other guys, but if you have some investment money or perhaps your parents do and you want to become a part owner in our winery, it would greatly help us if we could buy this property so that Rodriguez is out of our hair."

"Um, Nick, you're talking about SEALs here. None of us are sitting on lots of cash," Coop said.

"Yeah, but some of us married right, Coop," objected Fredo.

Everyone laughed.

Nick continued. "We're not considering filing any lawsuits or getting any detainers or restraining orders, unless he starts acting out. And if he does, then we will go for that. So I'm asking for two things. First, I'd like to know if you or some of your family members or an acquaintance that you trust might be able to invest in the property when I go to negotiate with Mr. Rodriguez. The second thing is, if I should need it and you're not on deployment, could you come help like some of you did when Sophie's nursery was being put on the market."

That brought the guys to a solemn silence.

"There's a lot to do, but we don't want to shut down the operation and perhaps signal that we're weak. We want to keep it running, but I'd like to have lots of eyes and ears everywhere. I got farm hands who can shoot to kill anything that moves within five hundred yards."

That brought on some heavy laughter.

"It's true. We have waiters who pack. If you come up, I'd like help with some of the events we've planned, and eventually, I'd like some ideas as far as legally the things we can do to keep him from being tempted to act up. It would be nice if the district attorney would reopen the case. But she's not going to do that. I've already checked into it. Those of you who can, if you can come up and give us a hand, I'd feel a lot more secure."

Jameson raised his hand. "Have you had any contact with him at all?"

"Nope. I might have to go through his attorney or his realtor. But if I asked for a meeting, I think he'd agree to it. And I need to see what his mental state is. That's going to tell me a lot of what we need to do too. One of the other things we can do is document anything that happens that's sort of on the edge of being illegal. If he harasses or does anything at all to threaten my family or you or any of the people that work at the winery, we need to keep a running journal of that. If we need to, it might be something we'd use in court."

"Kyle, if we wanted to stay behind and help—I understand Mark's going to be doing that—is anybody else allowed to do that?" Danny Begay asked.

"Danny, no. I'm letting Mark go… well I'm still getting approval for it, but I'm letting him go because he and Nick were always best friends and have known each other a long, long time. He spent a considerable amount of time up there, and I think it's a good time for Mark, with the baby coming and all. And third babies sometimes come early. You never know. I think it would be good for him."

Kyle didn't look at Mark, but the rest of the team immediately focused on him.

Coop was next to speak up. "Well, I think my father-in-law Austin Brownlee would be interested in investing. A few of us have a little bit of money saved, but most of us would probably recommend our parents. We've got some upper brass who might be interested. Armando's mother and Detective Mayfield might be interested. But I don't know. Anyway, I think we could get you a list of a few names, and let's just see how much we raise. Hopefully, it's enough."

"I was fortunate to conduct an operation that paid out well, and I think I'd be interested in stepping up, but I can't carry the whole load myself," said Brady.

Nick explained to the group. "Brady has a small piece of heaven up north of Healdsburg in the Dry Creek Valley. It's about a forty-five-minute drive from my property, in case you were wondering who this cretin is," Nick said.

Again, nervous laughter filled the room.

Fredo piped up next. "Shit, Kyle, let's just all fucking not go on this next deployment. I think we should all go up to Sonoma County. Is there any way you could pass this off onto Team 5 or one of the East Coast teams?"

"Not in your life, Fredo. We don't do that. That request would be career-ending. But we can help once we're back. And I have it on good authority this next deployment will be short, perhaps only thirty days."

The meeting was over quickly, less than twenty minutes. When Nick was done, he had a list of six investor names, including Brady. None of the team guys were in a position to donate or become investors, but nearly all of them wanted to help when they got back, the only exceptions being the two SEALs who had babies due close to that time.

Nick appreciated the support he was receiving. He had his army. He had a funding mechanism, or almost did anyway. All he needed was to uncover Rodriguez's motivation.

That was going to be next.

He needed to look at this son of a bitch eye to eye.

Then he'd know for sure.

CHAPTER 8

NICK WAS DELIGHTED to be home, delighted to be surrounded by his girls, and although he was extremely tired, he loved the fact that Devon had arranged for an overnight so that the two of them could have some personal time together. He learned about her plans midway between San Diego and Sonoma County.

"Now you're going to make me get a ticket, Devon. I can't wait to see you again."

"Well, I hope you accomplished what you needed to. I just thought we could use a little alone time. You're going to be busy these next few days, I know. There really isn't any updates on what's been going on, but people will start arriving tomorrow morning, trying to make suggestions and get your attention. So I just thought I'd put in my bid first."

Her sexy voice was music, absolutely stunning, a beautiful symphony to his ears.

"Devon, you are the smartest woman in the whole wide world. I don't know what I would do without you. You're a lifesaver. You're everything I don't deserve."

"Just get your butt up here. I'll take care of everything else."

His meetings down in San Diego had gone well. He'd met with Dr. Brownlee, who agreed to put together a group of some of his fellow physicians and wealthy customers in the area, even contacting his personal stockbroker, who assured Nick it would be relatively easy to raise the capital to expand the winery.

Nick observed that Dr. Brownlee was looking younger, more fit, and more tanned, apparently playing more golf or spending more time at the beach and not keeping those long office hours that consumed his energy. He let slip he'd been traveling to Europe, and rather than attending conferences on PTSD or psychiatry for the military, his specialty, he'd been on vacation.

Nick didn't get to meet his new love interest and felt it wasn't appropriate to even bring it up. He wasn't sure he was supposed to know about that.

Before he left, Kyle wished Mark good luck, giving him the full approval he needed to travel up to Sonoma County at the beginning of the following week.

Pieces of the puzzle kept slipping into place, one by one. Opportunities opened up, and problems were overcome or set on the right course. It wasn't going to be hard filling the spots he had available with team guys who were either injured or, for one reason or another, weren't selected for the mission. Kyle was selective on who he took, often not taking the whole platoon. It was his way of sharing the load.

This time, the team was going to Mexico, completing several of the snatch and grabs they'd been doing with local cartels bosses involved in drug smuggling and human trafficking rings. There was an endless supply of drugs and cartel members, but Kyle shared with Nick that his team were now tasked with locating some of the bad guys coming over from Afghanistan, Iran, Russia, and several parts in Cuba, Central America, and South America.

They had more jurisdictional control in Mexico as a force than they would ever have in the United States. But that was what they signed on for. Nick admired how Kyle gelled the team, refocused on their training program, batted down all the objections to other people wanting to join Nick's little mission in Sonoma County, and focus on the mission at hand: to get bad guys outside the U.S. border.

It had been a long, boring drive up north. He didn't allow himself to get tired but stopped and picked up a coffee, some cheese, a couple protein bars, and an energy drink, which he was hoping he wouldn't have to take.

THE SUN HAD set roughly half an hour before he turned off Highway 101 and headed down Bennett Valley Road to his piece of paradise. The sky was a bright turquoise blue, devoid of a moon. Stars started popping through the canvas of the dome above him, twinkling in the early evening air and adding their special brand of ambience, along with the chirping crickets.

The weather was mild, no rain in sight, as he pulled up to the gate, clicked his automatic opener, and smiled for his camera. He'd take a look at that cheesy grin when both he and Devon could have a good laugh over it, since it would be sent to his computer.

He proceeded through the entryway and down the gravel road to their house. The big wedding pavilion in the background was lit up, columns highlighted with flood lights hidden in rows of lavender. The huge silk curtains gently billowed in the breeze. It was quite a spectacle.

Their home was always being remodeled, since they found their needs changing with the ages of the girls. It was of modern design, something he might see in Colorado or Wyoming buried into a hillside at the base of a ski slope. The tall square frame had huge windows and a roll-up garage door in the living room, which accessed a marble-like, poured slab ground which usually was their outdoor dance floor.

Ultra-modern furniture dotted the house in bright colors. Devon loved shopping at Italian leather stores and sample shops. She'd done a marvelous job and could have been an interior designer, he thought.

But all these thoughts suddenly escaped him when he saw his beautiful wife wearing a very see-through negligee, leaning against their front door. She was framed by two ten-foot olive trees, backlit to highlight the meticulous hand trimming Devon had carried out.

He turned off the truck and stared at her surrounded by the magic of the place they lived, and one more time, he felt grateful to be so lucky to have such a life.

She posed for him several times, moving her hips back and forth, smiling, pulling her hair up on top of her head and then letting it down to fall upon those luscious shoulders. She fanned herself, making a mockery of the smoldering look he gave her.

Message delivered, sweetheart.

One of the best things about their relationship was their art of non-verbal messages, especially of the sexual and erotic kind.

His heart was beating wildly. He was eager to taste her.

She brushed the hair from her forehead, leaning forward, slightly bent at the knees, letting him see more cleavage than he had a right to see.

It was a definite call to action. He scrambled to get himself out of the truck, his hard on so big he could hardly walk.

So he ran and nearly tripped in the process.

Within seconds, she was in his arms. Leaving everything in his truck as he moved her into the house, he still had the foresight to at least lock it with a click before refocusing on her soft lips and the tiny beads of sweat lining her forehead. He removed his shirt as she waited for him to remove her nightie.

"God, I feel like a high schooler. I can't get my clothes off fast enough, Devon. Help me out here."

"You poor dear. You're going to fall over your shoes and tip over your pants getting them down to your ankles."

He was hopping all over the floor, had kicked off one shoe but struggled with the other canvas loafer older than God. Next difficulty was getting his right leg out of his pants without losing his balance. His package was so large it threw off his center of gravity and nearly sent him to the floor at her feet.

Bare chested, he hopped and this time was successful in getting his pants down. Panting and in great need of relief, he stood before her in his red, white, and blue boxers, his forever underwear he'd told her on their first night together, adopting the uniform most of the other guys on SEAL Team 3 did, always patriotic, always red, white, and blue, always stars and stripes, and always with a full to bursting package inside.

She slipped her fingers into his waistband and slid his shorts down, her fingers sending a chill down his spine, as he became fully exposed and gracefully stepped out of them.

Grabbing her in his arms again, he unwrapped her body from the flimsy pink fabric, knelt at her front side, and placed his cheek against her belly. Hugging her, his arms wrapped around her buttocks when he whispered, "Home. Thank God, I'm home."

Her fingers lazily sorted through his sandy light brown hair. She was patient, waiting for him to make the move. Her breath was soft, her scent intoxicating, her fingers probing, rubbing, and exploring him.

"I thought you said you were going to take charge?" he asked, mocking her earlier comments.

"Oh, I'm going to take charge all right. I just wanted to wait until you were completely naked and perhaps you've had a glass of champagne, or would you rather have some beer?"

"I don't need anything, Sweetheart. I want you." He stood, looking over her beautiful body, still firm and exciting and fresh even with the tiny belly she still had from her pregnancies. The woman he'd met as a virgin had become his muse, his temptress. He had been so experienced, and yet she floored him, slayed his heart, wrapped him up in stitches, and wouldn't let him go.

He didn't want to be anywhere else.

Naked, she led him to the kitchen where she poured him some Merlot champagne. It was part of their limited vintage, an experiment, and it turned out to be delicious.

She inhaled, staring into his eyes. Her honest gaze left him even more urgent and desperate.

She whispered, "To us, forever and ever. Our destinies were always entwined. I love you more now even as I love the girls, as well. I love you more because you sacrificed everything for me. You came back to life after Sophie. You've been my protector, my partner in business and parenting. You steadied the course. You made everything that I do ten times better. I don't ever want this to end, Nick."

"It never will, sweetheart. I promise you that. And you know, I keep my promises."

CHAPTER 9

NICK RECEIVED WORD early the next morning that Enemario Rodriguez agreed to meet with him to discuss their future plans. He had put the carrot out to his neighbor that perhaps there could be some kind of collaboration, that Nick desired to bury the hatchet, create a "fresh start."

He and Devon talked about it at length, and although it might be taken as a sign of weakness, he decided to play down any bravado or threats of violence or fights. He wanted Mr. Rodriguez to think that he'd given up, and in fact, he did want peace more than he wanted violence. But the giving up wasn't going to be what Mr. Rodriguez expected.

He dressed in business attire, wearing jeans and a sports jacket, no tie. Devon brushed the back of his navy-blue blazer, making sure he looked successful, clean, and confident. The way she sent him off with a kiss and a promise for more play time this evening left him in a really good mood, ready to conquer the world.

Rodriguez had agreed to meet in his attorney's office in downtown Santa Rosa, which was perfect for Nick. The firm specialized in vineyard management contracts, investment partnerships, and acquisitions. He was a specialist in real estate law, as well as bankruptcy, but he was known for being a shark in the courtroom, someone most attorneys in town didn't want to come up against.

Nick's attorney offered to come with him, but again, he wanted to catch Rodriguez off guard, even at the risk they caught Nick off guard. But since the setting was professional and there would be witnesses present, he didn't feel he was in danger. Obviously, there was something Rodriguez needed to tell him, and he knew Nick wouldn't meet with him alone.

He was riding the elevator to the top floor when he recognized a couple of Devon's former colleagues, realtors who used to work for the same brokerage. They rode up and got off at the floor just below without recognizing him.

Stepping out into the marble foyer, the wide expansive view of the Santa Rosa plain was breathtaking. In the early morning hours, the downtown buildings and steel ribbon of the 101 Freeway glistened like crystals.

An attractive receptionist in a black dress and very high heels addressed him.

"You must be Nick Dunn. Is that correct?"

Nick nodded, observing she had a little bit of red lipstick on her extremely white teeth. He decided not to tell her. "I'm here to see Mr. Rodriguez, and I believe his new attorney is Ernie Sanchez?"

"Mr. Sanchez has been called out on an emergency, a family issue. But we have Ernesto Della Majore sitting in today. Ernesto has worked with Mr. Rodriguez during the appeal process. He's very familiar with his case, as well as all the ancillary issues."

Nick wondered what the hell any of his appeal process had to do with their negotiation today, but he pretended not to make that obvious.

She ushered him into the glass conference room in the corner. Again, the views were breathtaking, with all four walls in glass. Two of them overlooked the downtown area, and the other two looked into the upscale office interior buzzing with activity. At the end of a very long slab of thick glass, sitting on top of a huge gnarled driftwood log that was sanded and varnished to perfection, Enemario Rodriguez sat, looking diminutive and smaller than Nick had remembered from before.

The gentleman sitting next to him was a big beefy man, and perhaps that's why Rodriguez looked so small. But Nick realized that spending eight years in prison was probably not conducive to a lifestyle of overeating and drinking, and he had to admit that Rodriguez did not look well. His eyes were shifty, darting back and forth, slightly red and rheumy, and his teeth were stained with nicotine. This really surprised him.

Della Majore stood up and grabbed Nick's hand, squeezing it, no doubt to make a point.

Nick reached across the table and offered his hand next to Rodriguez, who declined, showing both his palms.

"With the COVID, I do not touch anybody. I have been sick twice, and I do not want to get sick again. So you will forgive me please. I mean no insult to you," he said in his clumpy and highly accented English.

Nick shrugged. "May I sit?" he asked Della Majore.

"Of course, of course. I'm sorry."

Nick hunkered down in the uncomfortable leather wheeled chair with a squeak. All of a sudden, he began to get slightly nervous, realizing that he was in the presence of a desperate man. He'd often wondered how Rodriquez was faring in prison, and now he knew. He knew the man planned never to go back. He was a tamed and caged animal unexpectedly given his freedom, which he grabbed with both hands.

"So this is your meeting, Mr. Dunn. Please bring up what it is you wanted to speak to us about," Della Majore said with polish and confidence.

"Thank you—"

The attorney cut him off. "Just let me point out a couple of things first. There are no rules here, but if you would like, I could record the meeting." He held up a small recorder, showing his gold Rolex watch tucked just under his shirtsleeve. "I could have it transcribed and send a copy to you. As you elected not to have your attorney present, I feel it's only natural to offer you this service."

Nick knew the transcript would come with a hefty bill his own attorney would have a problem with, but he decided to agree to the recording anyway.

"Thank you, sir." As Della Majore clicked the small device, Nick laid both hands on the glass table top. Once again, he was interrupted by the receptionist, who brought in three bottles of cold water without asking permission first.

"Mr. Dunn, would you like coffee or some tea perhaps?"

"No, thanks. Water is perfect."

He watched the drips of condensation drizzle down the side of the plastic bottle and leave a small puddle on the table top. He halfway expected to be interrupted again. He knew attorneys liked to play cat-and-mouse games. No matter that they were highly polished, it was still gutter tactics. Nick reminded himself not to lose focus or spend too much attention on little details that were of little consequence.

He began his carefully rehearsed speech, pleading his case to the audience of two.

"So I have a proposal for you. I would like to move on with my life, and I'm guessing you're of the same mind," Nick said and waited for a reaction.

Like birds on a telephone wire, neither Rodriguez nor his attorney flinched or moved a muscle.

He cleared his throat, took a sip of water, and continued. "I thought that rather than resuming all the adversarial energies that consumed us before, we could amicably discuss a way we could part as friends."

Again, neither gentleman moved. Both shared the same expression, master poker players to a fault.

"Since your property is basically worthless without water rights, and I have no intention of diminishing our rights, I'm offering you a buyout, depending on how realistic and reasonable you are."

Nick watched as Rodriguez's eyes nervously scanned the room behind him on his left. It caused him to turn around and look, but he saw nobody there. The man was definitely odd. Something flashed in his eyes and then was gone in the same instant before he diverted his gaze. Nick wasn't quite sure how to read it.

Rodriguez nodded very slowly, as if the weight of his own skull was painful. In a raspy voice, he returned Nick's volley with one of his own.

"I was thinking it might work out the other way around. I thought, perhaps, with all of the unfortunate events that happened that you and your wife and children would prefer living in some other location, somewhere safe and perhaps less vulnerable?"

His tone of voice was conciliatory, but his eyes were cold, sending a shiver down Nick's spine. Now it was his turn to be stoic, but he really wanted to reach across the table and grab the guy's neck and twist it until he heard the vertebrae snap.

Enjoying the feel of the knife in his hand, Della Majore inserted himself.

"I'm sure we could come to some arrangement if you would just give us a price, Mr. Dunn," he added. "Mr. Rodriguez has had a lot of time to think about this during his incarceration. He stands to make quite a bit of money on a lawsuit we are filing against the Sonoma County District Attorney's office as we speak. We're suing the police department, their investigators, the coroner, and several other entities."

Nick understood the threat that perhaps his winery was one of those entities they had designs on including in the lawsuit.

"So what you're saying is you're planning to sue the county and whomever for what you perceive to be the wrongful incarceration of Mr. Rodriguez. And once that suit is settled, he would like to buy me out. Have I got that right?" Nick clarified, stringing it out further.

"Well, we both have choices to make. If you would rather live your remaining days there at the winery before it becomes financially unfeasible, embroiled in a lawsuit, perhaps many lawsuits, while constantly having your business interfered with and the source of your livelihood disrupted, that is your choice, of course. Mr. Rodriguez, on the other hand—"

"Excuse me, Mr. Della Majore," Nick asked. "What makes you think my business would be interfered with, that I would not have my tourist business? What makes you think that life at my winery and the wedding center that we've created would not be able to go forward? I have no intention of shutting down, chang-ing, or altering anything my wife and I have built. I'm merely offering you a solution, so you can set up a winery in a different location that has access to good clean water, instead of trying to find or truck in water."

"But you don't understand. I am the one who wants to buy you out," Rodriguez said with a sneer.

Nick was quick with the answer. "As you know, vineyards take an incredible amount of water. I under-stand you are planting fruit trees now, and that could be perhaps one solution. But you're forgetting one thing. I still have the water."

Rodriguez delivered a smile that once again chilled Nick all the way to the bone. He was about to say something when his attorney placed his hand on Rodriguez's forearm, indicating that he should stop. The attorney spoke next.

"We are going to be investigating the water source. It is a rather expensive process and may take several months. We may have to even do a wet weather perc or test boring wells to see where the source of the water actually comes from. You may be surprised to learn that, while the water may come from the well on your property, it may cross Mr. Rodriguez's property. That would give him water rights. *Complete* water rights. That would also give him the ability to use all of the water rights."

Nick's heart sank down to his ankles. He'd never heard of this scenario. He was nervous, worried that perhaps he'd overlooked something. He was going to have to consult a specialist, and if he had made a mistake and was wrong about his water rights, his entire future was at stake. Rodriguez seemed to relish the discomfort Nick was having, although Nick tried very hard not to show it. The smirk on the man's face made Nick's stomach roll.

Rodriguez leaned onto the glass top, forcing his head to extend as close as he could get it to Nick's body sitting across from him. "It may be, that rather than risk losing everything, you decide to sell to me, that way you absolve yourself and your family from all the painful, time-consuming, and expensive attorneys' fees, engineering fees, testing, and delays. We plan on putting an injunction against your use of the water. That's what I mean when I say your operation may be shut off, literally, at the spigot."

CHAPTER 10

LILLY'S SOFTBALL TEAM had carried on a winning season. Several months ago, they were invited to play in Orlando for a special tournament in their age group, competing with teams from all over the United States. Devon had been a softball champion in high school, but she did not coach Lilly's team. At the same time, she encouraged the girls, helped them with their practices, washed uniforms, straightened out transportation snarls, and made all the reservations for the trip to Orlando, which was coming up soon.

Nick wasn't sure they should still take the trip after his conversation with Rodriguez. He was also swamped, normal to the June wedding season, with several reservations that were going to occur during that time, back-to-back.

It was also a busy time in the vineyard, as the real work of vineyard management reared its ugly head. Fields were set to be plowed, sowing the mustard grasses into the soil before they fully bloomed. The vines had to be tied, pruned down to their strongest buds, and capped off. Nick spent a portion of his day training his new helpers on the proper care and feeding of the strong, gnarly plants, some of the older vines up to thirty years old.

And part of their training was showing the value of clean, sharp cutting tools. He insisted on doing his own sharpening with a stone, which saved them money but also suited his need for perfection. There was nothing more frustrating than cutting something stuck between the nippers, untangling, and reapplying alcohol to make sure no bacteria transferred to the new, clean cuts. He gave each of his helpers their own sharpening stone and a small spray bottle of alcohol to wear on their toolbelts.

This year, they were going to try bringing in goats to help with the weed control, adding organic fertilizer to the soil as the animals pulled and denuded the ground and hopefully not too much of the vines. He'd made an arrangement with a lady who produced organic goat cheeses for many of the restaurants in the area, as well as in San Francisco and down in the peninsula of Silicon Valley.

He'd ordered some exotic lavender plants from Israel, milkweed, and other flowering plants for hedges along the driveway which would help grow the butterfly population. The girls loved chasing them with their colorful nets. Nick gave them strict instructions on how to catch and release them without damaging their wings. They also loved searching for caterpillars to raise in their netted bags back at the house.

He knew the girls didn't know the difference their way of growing up was making on them. They'd discover it when they had children of their own, teaching them the basics of living organically, using hosts and beneficial pests to control some of the insects they needed to keep under control.

Everything was done without any chemical sprays. That often meant he had to share with the other creatures that crossed their land. But there was plenty enough for all of them.

It was good work. Hard but satisfying. Mother Nature didn't care about attorneys or that Rodriguez had brought danger and ripples of concern and uncertainty to his peaceful existence. Young couples still needed a place to get married. Births, deaths and the general celebration of life still had to happen, regardless of one man's obsession, and sense of revenge.

Every day, he pretended it was going to be his last, just like he did when he was active on the teams. He didn't want to miss any of it worrying about what could happen. He was going to make sure he and his family enjoyed as many moments as they had together, because even with the best of times, life was unpredictable.

The days swept by like the fall winds. Devon and Lilly were to leave tomorrow morning for the airport.

"Maybe Rodriguez will think about things a little bit now. It just doesn't feel like he's imminently going to go after us," Devon stated as she folded Lilly's freshly cleaned clothes.

"Remember when I told you not to underestimate the enemy?" he answered her.

"I don't disagree with you, Nick. I just think Lilly has such an opportunity to play in this tournament, something she'll remember her whole life. I hate to see her miss that just because we're afraid he's over there cooking up devious plans."

She was right, of course. He'd even said the same things about other situations where hesitation was not a friend to the forward march of time.

"I think it would be healthy for her to do it. Since you can't go, and I understand that, maybe I could take Mark or one of the other guys. I've already arranged to bring a couple extra mothers as chaperones. I don't understand how Rodriguez would even know we're gone, so we'd not be in any danger. Not unless you think this house is being bugged," she said.

"I think we're safe there, Devon. Let me see how Mark feels about it, but I'd have to send him out later.

He's not getting here until Friday. But it might work. Or one of the other guys. I'm positive I shouldn't leave. There's just too much going on with the winery, and if I'm called to another negotiation with Rodriguez again and I'm all the way in Florida, or if something happened here, I'd be too far away. And I think it's dangerous for both of us to be gone at the same time. I don't want you or the girls unprotected."

"But I'm just taking Lilly. You'll stay home with Laurel and Sophia. Maybe send Mark out in a couple of days, if he's willing."

It had already been decided before, but this was Devon's way of making sure Nick was fully on board. She'd even already invited one additional mother who couldn't go due to finances. Devon offered to pay for her way in full so she could watch her daughter be a star for the weekend.

The venue appeared safe, Nick mused. He read there were security guards, since it was an all-girls grammar school tournament, and oddly enough, the head of security was a former Team Guy. It was unlikely Rodriguez or any of his henchman would even know they were missing until they got back.

Nick admitted only to himself that he wished nobody had to leave his sight. And on the other side of that, just the thought of telling Lilly she couldn't go was too much for him to face. Of course, he could have never convinced Devon to keep Lilly home. She argued vehemently that would be too much of an intrusion into their ordinary life.

Because it was.

That evening, Nick helped her get Lilly ready. They bought her new cleats and a new ball bag. Her two sisters were extremely envious and kept begging to be included in the trip, but Nick put his foot down to stop the debate, and Devon backed him up. It was one thing for Devon to watch Lilly. It was not wise to have her help take care of the team and also to have to babysit her other two daughters.

It was a compromise. He felt it was a safe one.

Nick's attorney had helped with some research about the well and what Rodriguez had been threatening. He suggested that further communications go through the lawyers only, since Rodriguez had been so inflexible, giving off a dangerous vibe.

Nick was fine with that. He had a lot to concentrate on.

But the next morning, as Devon was to head for the airport, they were served with papers, a lawsuit implicating them in a conspiracy to frame Enemario Rodriguez in order to gain control over his property. The lawsuit also spelled out that Nick's sister, the previous owner, had purposely hidden information about the well. Their "extensive" research had indicated Sophie had directed her own well drillers to bury the results of the water source. Nick doubted that it could be true, but like any lawsuit, it was just one of the allegations they would have to refute. His attorney estimated the costs were mounting, and they were just getting started.

Nick consulted with Zak to find a good well driller, somebody with decades of experience who would have a collection of logs, to disprove their theory.

Devon was devastated with the paper served. Other than that, they'd had no communication with Rodriguez and very little work was done next door. So it was a surprise and caught everybody off guard.

Zak called to wish them luck.

"Nick, I think you're going to want to use Bernie Wyatt. He's the guy my neighbor used over here. It's a water-scarce area unlike the valley floor where you are. Bernie was able to find water with a witching wand, which my neighbor thought was kind of cool. But he's been a well driller for forty-five years. I think you can trust him. A lot of the other drillers in the county actually access his well logs and records, and he willingly shares them with anybody and doesn't charge for it."

"Thanks, Zak. Sounds like our guy. Did you ask him about what was being alleged?"

"Oh, he's rather crusty and noncommittal. He

doesn't want to get involved in the middle of it. He distrusts attorneys, and he told me he often pulls out of a job if he feels neighbors are being too unreasonable. So this is not really his cup of tea, but in order to arrive at the truth, he's willing to help us for a fee."

"I'm going to need a geothermal engineer, and I'm going to need a geologist. My attorney has given me a list of experts I'm going to have to call on. I'm worried about the price, Zak."

"I don't blame you, Nick. But let's just keep plugging on with it. If you can stop him at the court case, well, you know that's not going to stop him overall. He'll do something else then. So just hang in there, and let's just fight each battle one at a time."

He said goodbye to Devon and promised to update her if anything changed at home. He wished Lilly all the best. She was so excited she'd even slept in her uniform the night before they were to leave, and Devon had to wash it again this morning. She added it to Lilly's soft bag.

He addressed his daughter, kneeling in front of her. "Now, you remember what I talked to you about, Lilly. You don't talk to strangers, especially men. You stick close to your mother, and you never go anywhere where she can't see you or reach you quickly. Is that understood?"

"Yes. You don't have to worry about me, Dad. I

remember about observing things. I remember about knowing my surroundings, and I plan to have my baseball bat with me at all times. If anybody tries to hurt mom or any of the other girls, I'm going to whack 'em."

Nick was pleased with her energy and commitment, but it left a hollow feeling in his stomach. Something about the trip was beginning to bother him now with the service of the papers. But he chalked it up to having too much experience with the wrong types of people. He figured it was his imagination going wild.

They said their goodbyes. Nick held hands with his other two daughters as they waved back when their ride showed up and whisked them away.

Mark texted him to let him know that he was on his way, a day early, and would be arriving the next morning. Nick was pleased that he'd have some help. Several of Devon's colleagues from the office also agreed to take shifts babysitting if he needed it. A few of the women brought by a casserole and some bread, all things that Devon had arranged before she left.

The new lavender plants were placed in rows after having soaked for twenty-four hours. He watched as a couple of Zak's workers moved the small tractor up and down the rows between the vineyards. There was a crew that arrived to do some last-minute trimming and shaping for optimum grape production. He also made the decision to cut back some of the lavender, in order for them to spread out, bloom further, and have a richer harvest in the fall.

He gave an update to Kyle and then turned in early, reading stories to the girls until little Sophia fell asleep in his lap.

Just before he turned in, Devon called him, letting him know they'd arrived safely in Orlando. They'd tried to get the girls to go to bed early, but it was a lost cause. She and the other mothers loaded them up on pizza and other carbs until they finally gave out.

"Well, at least now you'll get some rest, Sweetheart," he said to her before he signed off.

But Nick knew dark days were ahead. He had so many questions and not enough experts to consult. Not enough money, either.

The crew was leaving late. Others were bunking down in the barn, and yet another pair were just beginning their shift. They'd be smoking and whispering in the night air while Nick tried the impossible: To relax and fall asleep.

Somehow, it would all work out. In the meantime, he remembered something Kyle had told him on one of his first missions with SEAL Team 3.

"Worry is the enemy of decision and forward momentum."

CHAPTER 11

MARK WAS IN great spirits when he arrived. Like Nick, he didn't like wasting any time with a hotel layover and drove straight through from San Diego.

His former teammate sauntered into the house, examining all the remodeling they'd done, and commented on how beautiful it was.

"When I heard about the fire, I was hoping you'd be able to rebuild and keep some of Sophie's eclectic decorating ideas. I'd say you did one up on her," Mark said.

"We rebuilt the pavilion too. Come take a look," Nick said as he led Mark out the rear kitchen double doors, across the patio, and down the meandering path to the wedding center itself.

Mark whistled. "Would you look at all that light! You can open this all up? These are garage doors, right?"

"They are. Really cool what a big space it opens up.

You can hold a huge crowd here, nearly three hundred for a seated dinner, more for a standup party."

"First class. Sophie would be proud, Nick. You really did her proud."

"We like to think she would be."

Mark was pensive all of a sudden. Nick guessed he was recalling Sophie's last days and how Mark had become her very brief love interest, sending his sister off with some warm caresses, kisses, and romance before her big trip home. He was forever grateful to his friend for doing that.

Though he wanted to, with Mark now married and expecting his third child, he deemed it inappropriate to bring it up, even if it was to thank him. His buddy knew Nick appreciated it, even though they hadn't spoken about it recently.

"Sophie was right," Mark whispered. "It is a slice of heaven up here." When he returned Nick's gaze, his eyes had watered, one tear streaking down his left cheek. "Let's make sure he doesn't win, Nick. Let's keep this for Sophie."

THE GIRLS CAME home from Laurel's soccer practice, brought by one of the team moms. Corey's daughter and Laurel were the two strongest players on the soccer team and, during the school year, nearly inseparable. She asked to speak to Nick while Mark wrestled with the girls on the living room floor.

"What's up?" he asked.

"You told me about your history with the neighbor, and I was keeping a special eye out for anything that was out of the ordinary," Corey said.

Her comment sent a chill down his backside. He swallowed and tried not to look nervous. "Okay, and…?"

"It could be just my imagination, but I think I stumbled on someone who appeared to be taking pictures of the team on the field, our team, not the team from Davis."

"Where was this person, and why did you feel it was inappropriate?"

"He was sitting quite a distance away, on a picnic bench over on the far side of the parking lot, near the entrance to the clubhouse at the golf course. He was using a telephoto lens. If he was really interested in taking pictures of our girls, like an interested parent or grandparent, he'd be on the sidelines, wouldn't he? He'd want to be close to get a good close-up shot, capture an expression. But this guy almost looked like he was taking pictures but trying not to be caught doing so."

Corey was right. Nick was certain Rodriguez had sent someone to either intimidate or to spy or perhaps surveil his girls. This had opened up a new phase of this drama, and he didn't like any part of it.

He really didn't want to know, but he had to ask.

"What did this man look like?"

Corey wrinkled her nose and sent a crease to her upper brow, pursing her lips. "I've never seen him before at the field. He was maybe thirty, kind of nondescript. Dark hair, but he wore a baseball cap and dark glasses. That's what spooked me, because most photographers I know remove their glasses when they shoot, since it distorts the image and makes it hard to focus. But he was half-hidden behind a large shrub, sitting on those green picnic tables the club put there in the shade."

Nick couldn't decide if he was relieved it wasn't Rodriguez himself, but it didn't help if it was some other pervert or a hired investigator up to no good.

"What was he wearing?"

"Jeans, white sports shoes, and a light-yellow golf style shirt. Nothing remarkable." She shrugged. "Am I going crazy, Nick?"

He feigned a lack of worry, but inside, he was churning.

"I think you're one of the sanest people I know, probably better than I. But we do have to keep our eyes and ears tuned for anything, so I'm glad you told me. I hadn't considered the girls would be of interest to them. I hope I'm wrong."

"Of course, it isn't against the law to take pictures, is it?"

"That's right. Free country."

"What do you suppose he was doing there?"

Nick didn't want to answer Corey. He sidestepped her question completely. "Would you recognize him if you saw him again?"

"I think so. Maybe you should come to the game on Sunday. I'll be there, too, and together, we can both scope out the place."

"Good idea. Let's plan on that. Or do you want me to do you a good turn and pick up Raylene on the way. I could drop her back after the game."

"Thanks, but I think I'll stay out of this one, Nick. I'll help you identify him, if I can. But until things blow over, I'm going to distance the girls, just in case."

Her comment took him aback. He took several deep breaths to calm his heartrate.

"Can't fault you for that, Corey. I hope it's just something innocent, but I can't afford to take chances, either. We do what we do to keep our families safe. I'm going to err on the side of caution."

"Thanks, Nick, for understanding. I want to help. I really do. I'll find a way to do that and still keep Raylene safe."

"Just be those extra sets of eyes and ears for me, Corey. Tell me if you see anything like this again."

He was disturbed when they walked inside the living room to the whooping and hollering of the three girls on the floor. Corey collected her daughter, and he sighed.

There was so much at stake, Nick thought. He was second-guessing his reluctant decision to allow Devon to take Lilly on her own to Orlando. It was so far away and she didn't know anyone there.

Have I just made the biggest mistake of my life?

CHAPTER 12

NICK GOT COLIN Riley's phone number from Brady after he revealed what Corey had told him about the sighting of the cameraman at Laurel's soccer game.

"Jeez, Nick, it's too weird to be a coincidence. Good thing you've got everybody looking out for you, but I don't know, man. It kind of feels like it's getting out of control. And how the hell did you let Devon take Lilly all the way across country?"

"I'm wondering the same myself, Brady."

Nick wasn't happy with some of the decisions he'd made, just a few of them anyway. But he knew he had to face everything straight on, tell the truth, evaluate it, and then not beat himself up for the repercussions. That was an easy thing to say and a difficult thing to actually carry out.

"I'll let you know what he says, Brady. You and Riley interested in a little adventure? That is, if it comes to that?"

"Oh boy, now you're making me think about things that are going to cost me my marriage, Nick. I can't very well leave you undefended, but want my opinion? For what it's worth, well, I'm not going to say it on the telephone, but you know there's another solution to all of this. You're going to stress yourself and everybody else around you half to death if you don't take care of it. One way or the other, Nick, you got to deal with it."

Nick knew exactly the unspoken intent of Brady's comment. They were both smarter than to voice something like that on the telephone where it could be overheard, and it made him even more anxious to get hold of Colin Riley. He also knew that, in a pinch, he could count on Brady. He'd catch hell for it, but it was something any of them would do for each other. It might as well have been in the Book of Uniform Commands, a rule set in stone. Everybody knew it existed but didn't talk about it openly.

Colin Riley's housekeeper, a former cook on the USS Zumwalt based in Coronado, answered the phone.

"This is Kevin, right?" Nick asked.

"I'm sorry, but do I know you?" he asked.

"You're Kevin, the kid from Nebraska who grew up on a pig farm and does a mean barbeque. You were stationed in Coronado while I was on SEAL Team 3. This is Nick Dunn."

"Holy shit. What a small fucking world."

Nick was glad that even though Kevin was obviously more like a celebrity chef and butler to billionaire and wheelchair-bound Colin Riley and his unique needs, he still had not lost his naval language. It was important to keep that part of the culture alive, even if he did sleep on silk sheets and have Gucci pajamas these days.

"So I got a little conversation I need to have with Mr. Riley. Is he around?"

"As a matter of fact, he's downtown, getting a little procedure."

"Is it serious?"

"Not really. A little skin cancer. He gets those. He also gets little things that pop up due to his being confined to that rocket that does everything but fly. Poor guy is a fighter, though, I'll tell you that."

"I don't want to get into too much of it, but he's still active, right?" Nick asked, referencing what he knew to be Riley's efforts to put together a paramilitary group for hire—something that could be used in case they had to have one hundred percent deniability, a force well trained with guys willing to go at it and occasionally cross the line. It was always something that a certain percentage of their SEAL community was drawn to. It wasn't anything Nick particularly wanted to adopt. But he was glad *somebody* was.

"Well, somebody's got to do the hard stuff, right?"

he said.

"Roger that."

"So he'll be back in about, oh, I'd say an hour or so. I'll have him call you."

Nick left his number and then signed off.

His next call was to return Devon's.

"Hey, Sweetheart. How is she doing?" he asked.

"Oh my gosh, Nick. She's having the time of her life. And today she had a home run with two on base. She loves softball, even asked me if I would teach her how to pitch, and shoot, Nick, I was a fielder. I don't know anything about that. So I think we're going to need to find somebody who can coach her. What do you think?"

"That's great sweetheart. Our little athlete. Well, she comes by it honestly with your background, Devon."

"I just hope everything works out so that we can afford something like that. I would give up five years of vacations to hire a really good coach for her. They give out scholarships now for softball, especially some of the small schools. It could be a good way for her to pay for her college."

"I'm game. We'll look into it when you get back."

"Thank you! I was worried you'd say no."

He let a few breaths in and out before continuing. "So I want to give you a brief update on what's going on here. Corey gave me some news today I didn't really relish hearing. She said there was someone at Laurel's soccer game taking pictures today."

"Well, they take team pictures all the time, Nick. You know that."

"No, not like this. She said she thought the person taking the pictures was trying to hide, trying to either do some kind of surveillance or take close-ups of the girls, and I'm not saying it's a close-up of Laurel, but he had a telephoto lens, Devon. I mean, Corey said he looked like he was hiding behind a bush, perhaps wearing a disguise. You would think if it was a team photographer or a father or an uncle trying to get some action shots that he'd be on the sidelines where you could get expressions, because that's where all the action is, isn't it?"

"I see what you mean. So what are you going to do about it? Did anybody else see him?"

"I don't know, but I'm going to go on Sunday and watch. She and I will carefully scope out the environs just in case he shows up again. If he doesn't, well, that doesn't mean we're in the clear, but I guess I'd be a little relieved. And if he is there, I want to find out who he is and what he's up to."

"You should take Mark with you if he's there."

"Yep, he arrived. The girls are delighted. He's told them he's going to take them to the Sonoma County

Fair. It's like good old uncle Mark, always a ladies man, right?"

Devon mused on that a bit and yawned. "It's three hours later here, so it's 11:30. I pulled the girls out of the pool here at the hotel about a half an hour ago. If I had let them, they'd swim all night and then play like hell in the morning."

"Where are they in the standings?" Nick asked.

"Well, there are four flights of four, and they have won one game and tied one."

"Tied, don't they go into overtime? Extra innings?"

"Not for the younger girls. They only play six innings. And at the end of six, that's the score. I think for the final game they let them go up to nine innings, but I'm not sure. She's playing much younger than I did, and next year, she can play up a couple age groups."

"That's music to my ears. Are they at the top of their flight?"

"I think they are tied with another team, but tomorrow's games will cinch it. After the first game, they'll reshuffle, and all the first- and second-placed teams will be in a flight of eight. Then they'll start sudden death elimination after that. It's really well organized. And although they're being very competitive, the girls are getting along great, even the girls from the other teams."

Nick remembered his own days as a Little Leaguer,

and he guessed the way Lilly's softball team was operating was much healthier.

"My dad would beat the shit out of me if we lost. It was like life-or-death, because that's the way it felt growing up. You know he didn't have any parenting skills. It's a wonder I turned out."

"You not only turned out, Nick, but you're a great dad. I've had mothers come up and talk to me about how good you are with the girls. So many of these girls have fathers who never show up. It's almost half. I just don't understand that."

"Well, those are the people who are letting everybody else raise their kids. I'm not going to do that. We're not going to do that, right?"

"Absolutely correct. I'm not onboard with that," she said.

"Well, I better let you go. You give her my love and just keep watching everybody around you guys. Maybe set your sights a little farther? I don't think that Rodriguez knows about your trip, but he had to have found out about Laurel's soccer game. If he knows that, then perhaps he knows about Lilly's softball. And that bothers me, mostly because you're clear across the country. I can't just drive over there and be there in a half an hour."

"I'm glad you told me, but don't stress over it, Nick. We've got it locked down here so tight. They're not letting even brothers and cousins come watch unless they stay in the stands, and there's gated entrances that are secured with guards. You can't walk on the field like you can a regular softball game. It's a regular professional field, Nick. They're used to dealing with rabid fans who get crazy, so a bunch of girls out there having a good time and playing their little hearts out, it's just not the same vibe. I think she's safe, and I'm very grateful she has this experience. Who knows, maybe I would've become a professional softball player instead of going into real estate if I'd had these opportunities."

"But, sweetheart, I'm really glad you did. We wouldn't be nearly doing so well if you weren't bringing in that income. You're doing exactly what you needed to do."

"Okay, okay, I'll give you a call tomorrow after the game, and I think Lilly would probably like to talk to you, too, unless it's horrible news. She talks about you constantly, Nick. There's 'Daddy this' and 'Daddy that.' She tells the girls everything about you. She tells the girls about how brave you are, what a hero you are, and how handsome you look in your dress whites. I've never heard her speak so excitedly about you. And she even told them how you had her swinging a bat at pumpkins and hitting fence posts and trees. How to kick and hit and scratch. They were giggling in the pool as I overheard those conversations. You would have loved it. Even with all of this crap going on, this has been a really great experience for her. Something she'll remember for the rest of her life. And I'm still going to keep an eye out around me, but I think the real action's going to take place in Sonoma County. So don't worry about us. We're good."

"Devon, you're more than good. You're the best."

Shortly after he hung up, Colin Riley returned Nick's call.

"It's been a long time, Nick," Riley said. His voice was scratchy and a little shaky. Nick figured in his head how old Riley must be and guessed he must be in his upper-seventies now. The years were taking a toll on the brave man in the wheelchair.

"Sir, I apologize for being a ghost. We've been busy, and we've done very well. As a matter of fact, I'm working on putting together an investor group to try to purchase the property next door. And that's the reason for my call."

"You're calling for money? I'm a little surprised."

Nick chuckled. "No, not really. I'm trying to buy out my neighbor next door, you know the guy that was responsible for killing my sister? They got him out of prison on one of those innocence projects. Tossed his conviction out, and after eight years, he's free as a bird. He's still fixated on owning my property, and I'm not sure if you realized this or not, but he's out of water, and I have a huge well that probably could water half of Santa Rosa. I approached him after talking to a few of my buddies' parents and getting the go-ahead to offer him some numbers we were hoping he'd take. It's a no-go, Mr. Riley. The guy is even more fixated on my property than he was before, when Sophie was alive."

"So you've got a problem then, is that right?" Riley said.

"Yes, sir, I do. So I wanted to ask your advice, and I want to try to end this peacefully. I know now it won't be amicable, but I need to get him out of our lives. I was just told today that somebody was at the soccer field taking pictures of my middle daughter's team. That worries me."

"It should. You know who the guy is?"

"I didn't see him. One of the mothers told me. But I'm going to show up on Sunday and see if I can spot him."

"You think maybe this guy is hired by your neighbor?"

"My hunch is, yes. Now you tell me, Riley, am I being paranoid?"

Colin Riley sucked in air and then blew it out. Nick noticed his inhale and exhale was more labored than he remembered the last time he saw him.

"When it comes to our families... you know my

story about my son," Riley said.

"Yes, sir, I do. I'm so sorry about that."

"Well, you guys got my daughter out. I owe your team a lot, even though you weren't on that op. But when it comes to our families, our loved ones, there isn't any such thing as a price too high to pay. Extreme measures sometimes get required when it has to do with our family. I think you better make the decision that, once you verify everything, you don't hesitate. You make a decision, and you act immediately."

Nick's belly did flip-flops. His heart began to race. He knew Colin Riley had a sixth sense about such things, even though he'd never served on a SEAL team before. But he thrived on inserting teams into dangerous places and pulling off the impossible, with a combination of unlimited funds, specialized equipment, and hiring the very best trained men and women. This was as close to the confirmation Nick was also leaning towards as he was going to get.

"I got your message loud and clear. I guess the next step is the confirmation then. I don't want to do anything to jeopardize myself or my buddies. But I don't think there's a snowball's chance in hell of Enemario Rodriguez fading into the sunset."

It was Riley's turn to chuckle. "Well, maybe we can help with that."

CHAPTER 13

THE GIRLS WERE jumping up and down early in the morning, waking both Nick and Mark up, anxious to go to the Sonoma County Fair per Mark's promise. Nick explained that the best time to go was early in the morning, because by afternoon, it could get very warm and dusty. Plus, there was a considerable difference in the population of fairgoers as it got closer and closer to dinner time and then evening.

Generally, families with small children went in the morning.

Because they were both veterans, they were given a ticket for half price. Sophia and Laurel were free since they were both under ten.

Nick knew the girls would want to go straight to the animal section, where displays of unusual chickens and roosters, baby lambs, rabbits, and ducklings were all housed. They even wandered down between the rows of sheep and cattle raising done by various 4H boys and girls. He pointed out to Sophia how spotless and clean the lambs were. Electric trimmers could be heard all over the buildings. Their hoofs were sanded and polished. Handlers even brushed their teeth. Both girls were fascinated with all the attention the animals got and how pampered and perfect they looked when the 4Hers were done.

"What do they do with them after the fair's over?" Laurel wanted to know.

Nick was going to be honest with her, but he wasn't quite sure how Sophia would react. "Well, Sweetheart, they auction them off and people bid on them. They pay by the pound, and then the animal is slaughtered, and oftentimes, the meat is donated to homeless shelters and soup kitchens. It's a donation for the people who are supporting the 4Hers."

Sophia looked up at him with her eyes in distress. "They kill them, Daddy?"

"Yes, Sweetheart. They're learning how to fatten cattle and little sheep for market. It's training on how to be a good farmer. And although the end result is usually the same, these animals are cared for and loved. They were raised for food, not as pets."

Sophia's little chin rested on the top of the metal gates as she watched a young girl gently brush and fluff a docile and very fat ewe. Her eyes began to blink quickly, and Nick knew she was about to cry. He put his arm on her shoulder.

Mark discovered a pen of pregnant goats. Several of the mothers had already given birth, and the baby goats were jumping, running through their food and their water, extremely unruly but fun to look at.

"I want a baby goat, Daddy," said Sophia. "Can't we have one or maybe two? Maybe we could learn how to take care of goats. We could have one for all of us."

"Well, I'm not about to make that decision without your mother's input. She'd have my hide if she objected. They are a lot of work to care for. But let's see what she says when she comes home, okay?"

Her bright smile nearly spread from ear to ear. Laurel was also jumping, clapping her hands together.

"That would be awesome!"

As the girls continued to walk between the stalls, Mark whispered in his ear, "You're absolutely crazy, Nick. You better not do that. I understand goats eat everything. Think about how beautiful Devon's flower gardens are. Those guys get in there and could probably level it in, you know, less than ten minutes. She's not going to like that."

"I didn't promise, just for the record," Nick reminded him.

The last building they came to housed all the fowl. They had a small plastic wading pool with ducklings swimming back and forth, and the children were allowed to come inside the gate and gently pick them up. Sophia examined her little white duckling, and she put her nose very close to the duckling's beak, speaking to him in baby talk. Suddenly, the little creature reached up and bit her nose, which didn't hurt her but scared her to death. She fell back on her seat and dropped the duckling, who flapped its baby wings and got himself right back into the pool with his other friends.

They examined the plumage on several large roosters, in unique colors like salt and pepper or sometimes iridescent silvers. Some of the roosters had spurs, others had yellow legs, and still others had greenish or white legs. The birds were also judged on their size, overall weight, and the variety and color of their plumage.

Beyond the roosters were individual cages with laying hens in them. That was actually something Nick had been considering, since having fresh eggs was something Brady had been boasting about, and they'd actually been given fresh eggs from time to time from his farm. He showed Sophia and Laurel the blue and green eggs and even found a purple one. At the very end, a fat speckled black and white hen laid chocolate brown eggs.

"Cuckoo Marans!" said Mark. "Would you look at those? Those eggs are so pretty. They look like chocolate, don't they?"

"Daddy, I want to have a chocolate chicken laying chocolate eggs. Can we do that please, please, please?" Sophia begged him.

"I'm going to go out on a limb here and tell you I'm in favor of it. I think it would be very healthy, and chickens are much easier to take care of than goats or sheep. I don't think your mom would mind. But we still have to ask her permission."

"Can we watch them hatch?" his youngest asked him.

"I think that can be arranged. We just have to find the eggs that are fertile, so that they will hatch. Not every egg becomes a chicken or a rooster. You have to find special eggs to hatch baby chicks."

They wandered through the myriad of colorful tents, hucksters selling chances at throwing darts at balloons, tossing ping pong balls onto glass plates, or trying to sink a ping pong ball into a tiny fishbowl. There were rides interspersed, even a Funhouse, with wavy mirrors and all sorts of creepy sounds coming from it. Laurel wanted to go inside, and Mark agreed to take her through. Nick and Sophia waited on a painted bench outside.

He checked the surroundings, looking for somebody who was a little too interested in them, and didn't see anything that was out of the ordinary. He watched the carneys, observing them hustle a buck here and there from passers-by. They encouraged little children to try their hand at tossing baseballs or hitting a target with a potato gun. Sophia was patiently waiting on his lap, her eyes glued to the exit of the Funhouse.

"You having a good time, Sophia?" he asked.

"The best. I can't wait to tell Mommy."

Nick eyed his watch and reminded himself that Devon was supposed to call him after they had their morning game. He checked his phone to make sure the ringer was on, so he wouldn't miss that call. Just as Mark and Laurel exited the house, his phone did ring. But instead of it being Devon, it was his attorney, Winston Harris.

As Sophie ran to join Mark and Laurel asking questions about the Funhouse, Harris caught Nick up-to-date on some of the legal proceedings going on between his neighbor and him, as well as the county and several other entities.

"I'm going to file, with your permission, for a dismissal of the lawsuit. It's really without merit. There's no basis for it and no proof. It really isn't appropriate in a civil matter, since interfering with his enterprise would be a criminal event, chargeable by the district attorney. They don't have the stomach for such a thing, and Rodriguez's barracuda of an attorney is shaking the trees just to see what falls. He might even get a settlement from them, but I don't think there's any basis for you to worry."

"That's good to hear. Finally some good news."

"Well, it's not a sure thing, Nick. And this is just one crazy case. I mean the guy was practically caught red-handed in a murder, and he has the nerve to accuse you of interfering with his farming operation. That's just nuts. I'm going to recommend his attorney be cited for giving rather poor judgment. But it wouldn't be the first time an attorney has done something just so he could earn some extra fees. We'll see how it sorts out."

"What about the engineering and the water analysis, the source of the water. Have you talked to the well driller?" Nick asked.

"He hasn't returned my calls yet. He was out there, what, yesterday? Or was it the day before?"

"Two days ago, Winston. He's got the old well logs, and he's not sure what kind of evidence they're going to present to prove what source the water is coming from, but he doesn't appear too worried about it."

Nick added, "I guess we just have to wait and get his report. Is there any chance I can get reimbursed for some of this? I mean, if the charges against me are thrown out, wouldn't they have to reimburse me for all these specialist fees and special reports and surveys?"

"That depends on how it happens, Nick. And we're

still in a fact-finding mode here. Now is not the time to worry about the fees. We need to do whatever we can to arm ourselves so they don't get any kind of a foothold or an inroad, a reason to interfere with *your* operation. And we absolutely do not want them to interfere with your water supply, either. We can complain and file a motion to make sure no drilling is done that affects your land, your water. Until they prove that it's actually sourced on his property, he won't be allowed to investigate it on yours."

"I'm a relieved with that. And I get what you're saying about the cost. I'm just trying to keep everything level. I've got extra people on my payroll. It's going to be months before I actually get a check for my lavender, and we're busy as heck with weddings for this month, but most of that was paid out to us six months ago when they made the reservations. I have really had a drop off for the winter time and next year. It's like people haven't jumped in and decided to set dates and all of that. I'm going to have to watch my pennies carefully."

"Are you still working on getting that investor pool together?"

"I am. I've got Dr. Brownlee, several of his colleagues, Brady, and various team guys with family money. So I was totaling up everything, and I think we could offer him five or six million. That's probably way more than it's worth right now without water. I just don't know."

Harris whistled. "Boy, I would think he'd take that money and run. He's definitely got something else up his sleeve, doesn't he?"

"I think he's a bit disturbed. Maybe confused. There's something not quite right about the guy."

They agreed to touch base again in several days, after Devon came back home from Orlando.

Nick watched Mark take the girls over toward the craft building, and Mark followed behind about five feet.

His cell rang again, and this time it was Devon's number.

"Hey, Dad, we won. We go on to the championship bracket," Lilly said.

Nick could hear girls cheering and lots of happy sounds as the team behind Lilly continued to celebrate while she talked to her dad.

"That's fantastic. Your mom told me how well you were doing last night. Was it a good day today?"

"The best. I got a double, and I got a triple. I didn't get any home runs today, but I did catch a fly ball. They had me working as catcher, too, which I'd never done before."

"Ah, catcher's a very important player on a team, aren't they?"

"Yep. They asked me about pitching, and I thought maybe mom could teach me. What about you? Daddy, can you show me how to do a softball pitch?"

"Your mom and I kind of talked about getting you a real coach. I could probably show you some things, but as far as technique for strikeouts and how to strategize how you play, I'm clueless when it comes to that. Your mom would actually be better than me. But we'll look into it. She's already asked me."

"I love it here. It's so warm, and the mothers have agreed that maybe we can go to one of the theme parks tonight after our play is done."

Nick had some reservations about that, mostly because if they were going to be in a theme park with crowds of people there and he wasn't there to watch, he felt they'd be walking into too much potential danger.

"And you're going to leave me behind?" he asked. Hoping she'd understand that angle, he pretended to be disappointed she wanted to go without him.

"We could go when you come. We could go to one of the places in California, which would be closer."

Nick agreed and, after congratulating Lilly one more time, asked if he could talk to her mother.

"Hey there, Sailor," Devon said in her sexy, buttery voice. "Looking for a good time?"

"Devon, that is not fair. But I'll get even when you get back."

"Promises, promises."

"So how did it go? Did they come out way ahead, or did you guys have some squeaker games?"

"Oh, that's an official softball term. Squeaker games. Where did you get that?"

"I made it up. You know that."

"Well, they annihilated their competition from their own flight. There was another really good team from, I think, Illinois and those girls were pretty tall. We were suggesting that perhaps they'd want to check the girls' date of birth. They looked like they were junior high age. They had some awesome hitters, but Lilly's team was able to hit off any pitcher they put up there. If they didn't have a weakness on their pitching staff, I think our girls would've been eliminated right off the bat. So they're now playing the best four from the other flight, and there's all good teams in that flight. The rest of the group in the eight flights is playing for the bottom half of the tournament. I'm very impressed with how it's run. And no issues, Nick. I feel very safe here."

Nick was relieved. "She wants to go to Disney World. She said some of the mothers have been talking about that? I'm not sure it's a good idea, Devon."

"I agree. But I'm going to go with whatever the group wants to do. If they want to take them over there for a couple of hours to walk until their legs fall off, I'll probably let her go. But only if we all go as a group, and only if we all go to the same areas, not split up all over the parks. I would think they'd be tired, because they played really hard, and it was hot today. But we'll see. We have the afternoon session, and that's going to depend on how that goes. We'll know about this evening. I, for one, would just absolutely love floating in the pool instead. But you know I'm probably going to be overruled."

"Well, you take care, and I'm going to go with the girls and Mark to Laurel's soccer game tomorrow. I'm going to go seek out this photographer that Corey discovered, and I'll let you know about that as well. So be good, Sweetheart, and remember, keep looking. Keep searching. Try to remember the faces of the people around you. Try to catch somebody staring at you or being too interested in what you and Lilly are doing. But I secretly hope that none of that occurs. I can't wait to get you home."

"Me too. Tell Laurel best of luck for tomorrow."

"Same to Lilly. Give her a big hug and kiss for me."

There was an awkward pause in their conversation, but Nick wasn't quite sure what he should say. So he added one last warning. "I do have guys I know who are stationed out of Norfolk. They'd be just a few hours away if something occurs. You make sure and not be unreasonable if something comes up. I want you to call me. Also, Winston says he thinks we'll get the charges in the lawsuit tossed out. It's not a for sure thing, just an indication. So things are looking good."

"Have you had a chance to talk to Colin Riley yet?"

"I have, and he's agreed to help us, whatever we ask."

"That's huge. With that guy and his team of experts on our side, Mr. Rodriguez doesn't have a chance."

CHAPTER 14

NICK CALLED BRADY and asked if he could accompany them to the soccer game coming up this afternoon. He told Brady he would feel a lot more comfortable if he could have just a couple more sets of eyes. It was Brady's suggestion they use one of his other workers too, a former police officer now retired. So they asked Wyatt to come with them as well.

Devon called with the happy news that Lilly's team was actually going to play in the finals, and they had elected not to go to one of the theme parks so they could be prepared for the big matchup. It was something all the parents and the team were extremely excited about. Nick was pleased the girls came to the decision on their own that they wanted to swim in the water and then go to bed early so that they would be fresh and prepared.

While he and Mark were helping get breakfast out, Sophia pretended to use her stuffed animals as chickens and ducks from her fun trip to the fair the day before. Both she and Laurel had picked up wristbands, handmade and woven with an attractive design in red and yellow strings. They were the types of wristbands that once you put them on and cinched them, you had to cut them to get them off.

"Where did you get these, honey?" Nick asked Laurel.

"Over in the crafts building, there was this man who was making these little wrist bracelets, and he gave it to us. He said it was good luck."

"I didn't see you talk to him. When was that?"

"Remember you were talking to the guy who made the model ships?" Laurel insisted.

Nick all of a sudden remembered the five minutes or so that both he and Mark were totally absorbed in the ship building prowess of this young artist. And he thought he was keeping an eye on the girls, but they had been walking back and forth between the tables, speaking to artists, and looking at their wares. He just never noticed they had the wristbands on until this morning.

"Well, I guess if it's going to be good luck, then your team's probably going to win today, right?"

"That's what he said. He said I looked like a soccer player."

Nick's bones went stone-cold.

He knelt in front of Laurel as Mark walked into the kitchen and saw them there. "What did this man look like?"

"He looked like somebody's grandpa. He was a nice man. He smiled. He didn't have very many bracelets, Daddy," Laurel finished.

"Remember when I talked to you about not talking to strangers? You shouldn't have talked to him. And you shouldn't have accepted this bracelet unless I was there. You can't be doing this, Laurel."

Sophia approached. "But, Daddy, it was free. We didn't have to pay for it."

"It doesn't matter. I don't want you talking to strangers. Nobody, that means nobody." Nick was insistent. He was a little bit irritated mostly with himself, but now he was certain they were trying to get to him through the girls. This escalated the stakes.

Instead of bringing just Wyatt and meeting Brady at the park, he had Wyatt's son accompany him, and then he also asked one of Zak's workers to ride with them. He was hoping it wouldn't be too obvious he'd shown up with a whole lot of extra security, but if there was a photographer there or someone who Corey recognized, he wanted to get some answers. He also asked the guys if they could take pictures themselves of whomever they might suspect could be someone that would be hired to do surveillance.

Before they left the house, Nick cut off both of the bracelets. He tossed them on the kitchen countertop.

Mark picked up one of the bracelets and studied it. The one that had been given to Laurel had a small silver charm on it, and it was about the size of a small St. Christopher medal, except it wasn't. It was a disc all right, but as Mark looked at it closer, he asked Nick for a pair of tweezers. Nick reached in the medicine cabinet in the bathroom and brought them out.

"What are you doing there?" he asked Mark.

"I thought this was just a little fastener of some kind, but now that I'm looking at it, it has a seam and—"

All of a sudden, the top of the disc flew off and hit the glass in the window, falling back into the kitchen sink. Both he and Mark peered inside what was left of the bottom side of the disc, and there was very clearly a computer chip resting in the middle—a tiny circuit board no larger than about a quarter of an inch. Mark used the tweezers, pulled the innards out, and looked at it again closer.

Nick started to ask more questions, and Mark put his finger up to his lips. Then he shook his head, and he asked if Nick had any empty Pyrex or glass jars. Nick handed him one from the lower cabinet, a food storage jar with a plastic lid that snapped down. Mark placed both halves of the device and the tiny circuit board inside, covered it, and snapped the lid shut. He walked into their storage room off the kitchen, placed it on the top shelf, and then closed the door, leaving it behind.

"What was it?" Nick asked.

"That's a very sophisticated tracking device, Nick. We're going to have to get that to somebody right away. It's not a good sign. I didn't see one on Sophia's band, only on Laurel's. I don't know what kind of a game he's playing, but this guy has just raised the stakes. We're going to have to report this to the FBI. Local Sonoma County Sheriff isn't going to be able to touch this with a ten-foot pole—it's way beyond them."

Nick sat down at the kitchen table, placing his forehead in his palm. "I'm sick about this, Mark. Should I be taking the girls and moving, living elsewhere?"

"I thought you wanted to appear not to do anything out of the ordinary. I thought you wanted to throw him off that way. We've cut this bracelet off her wrist, so he's going to know we discovered it. I'm hoping we can get some kind of information about what it is, who manufactures it, and where he could have gotten it from. But it's very clear somebody is tracking your daughter. Not you, Nick, your daughter."

Nick dialed Kyle's number and told him what they'd discovered.

"She got that at the fair?" Kyle asked.

"Yep. I don't know how it happened, Kyle, but it was just a couple minutes when Mark and I were checking out this incredible model boat builder. I was watching the girls out of the corner of my eye, but they were just meandering back and forth. I mean, I was only about ten steps away."

"So you saw him then?"

"I did, but it doesn't register that it was Rodriguez. He had the same build. Just the hair color's wrong. This guy had silver hair, but he definitely was about Rodriguez's size."

"Easy enough to find a wig, and he probably altered his look with the facial hair?" Kyle asked.

"Yeah, he had a mustache. A big white bushy mustache. Son of a bitch. Here I've been lecturing everybody about paying attention, and this guy was right there right under my nose."

Kyle mumbled a curse Nick could barely hear.

"So now what do I do? Who do I give this to?"

"I think you need to call Riley. He'll send someone down. He probably has someone that will recognize it right away. I don't want you making any more guesses, Nick. You've got to get some help here."

"Well, we're going over to the soccer game. I'm taking Brady, Wyatt, and Wyatt's son. We're going to scour that soccer field and look for that photographer or somebody who looks like Rodriguez."

"Where is Rodriguez staying, do you know?"

"One of the guys said they think he stays in the house over at the ranch next to mine. They've seen some black SUVs pull in and out. There're lights on over at the house. I've seen that. But as far as seeing him there, I haven't."

"So this is what you do, Nick. You follow this photographer or whomever else shows up today. You follow them home. You wait until he leaves, and then you search his house."

"Roger that, Kyle. That's a good idea. We're on it. And I'll keep in touch."

"Anything happening in Orlando?" Kyle asked.

"Everything seems to be fine there. I honestly don't see how he would know where Devon is. Lilly's playing in the championship game this afternoon while we'll be watching soccer. She's having a great time."

"Well, you're probably right about that then. But, boy, if she were my wife, Nick, I'd get her home just as soon as that game's over. I think it's a huge liability having them so far away by themselves with nobody to protect them. I mean, this guy is so crazy he doesn't even care that you know he's coming for you. And of course, he's doing it through your soft, gentle side… through your kids. You need to get Devon home. And then I think I'd recommend you guys move someplace temporarily."

"I'll talk to Riley, and then I'll let you know what we decide. But yeah, let's get this device looked at and analyzed. Then we'll know what we're dealing with."

The game started a little late because the park sprinklers all of a sudden came on, flooding one of the goalkeeper boxes. It took approximately forty-five minutes before the puddles of water drained into the soil, although most of the parents didn't seem to be very concerned. Nick knew it was not a coincidence this sort of thing was happening today.

He had searched the perimeter. Then he sent Brady and Wyatt up to the clubhouse to rent a golf cart and had them meander back and forth on some of the paths between the park, the clubhouse, and the course. Mark stood on the opposite side of the field and tried to look supportive of the other team, standing with parents, listening to conversations, and studying everybody's faces and where they were watching. From time to time, he would turn around and search the bushes or look over in the direction of the golf course and then draw his attention back on the game.

Nick was not able to focus, and Laurel had to ask him twice to wish her luck before he realized he'd been distracted.

"Oh, absolutely, Sweetheart. Your mom sends her love as well. They're rooting for you from Orlando.

And Lilly is playing her game at the same time."

"I think we're going to win, Daddy." She ran out into the field, and her team was given red jerseys to wear over their T-shirts to distinguish them from the other team. Nick stood by the sidelines in the middle of a group of fathers, clutching Sophia's little hand. She tried to wiggle loose several times, but he insisted that she stay right next to him.

Laurel's team scored two goals before Laurel scored one herself. The score was three to nothing at half time. His daughter was sweaty, her cheeks pink and her hair coming undone. Nick knew that Devon would have combed and braided her hair all over again, but he decided to let her play the part of a tomboy and left her just the way she was. She was athletic, tall for her age, and beautiful.

The referee blew the whistle twice, signaling the beginning of the second half of the game, and this time, the score was much closer, the other team scoring two goals within the first minute and a half. The parent group on Nick's side grew suddenly quiet. The other side had come to life.

He hadn't noticed Brady and Wyatt had followed the path on foot back to the park, and Wyatt walked up to him, whispering, "I found something, Nick. We found a guy taking pictures. Brady wants to follow him home. Not that I could stop him, but are you okay with that?"

"I am, and you can go with him if you want. You up for that, Wyatt?"

"It's what we do, Nick. So we're going to hang out here, and when he leaves, we leave. We'll let you know what happens."

"Roger that. Where the hell is he, anyway?"

"I want you to look to the right and nod to one of the mothers over there's who's jumping up and down. You see those three over there?" he said, pointing.

Nick leaned forward and nodded his head, smiling at the ladies.

"Okay, now I want you to look to the left across the parking lot, and you're going to see the duck pond. Right at the edge, you're going to see a guy standing with a backpack, and he's got his back turned to the game. But he's not going to stay that way. Don't look at him too long. When he starts to turn, you look away. We're taking pictures of him, not to worry."

Nick saw the fellow in a baseball cap, sunglasses, and wearing a set of khaki slacks and white sneakers, just like Corey had described. As Laurel's team scored another goal and the parents were cheering, he saw the man begin to turn, so he looked away. He walked with Sophia down past the midline, looking for Corey. She was standing next to her husband and gave him a smile.

"Corey, there's a guy over there by the duck pond. You recognize him as being the same one you saw two days ago?" he asked her. He had his back to the man, but Corey was facing him, and after studying him, she slowly nodded her head.

"That's him. That's the same guy."

"Thanks." He was going to say more, but the opposite team scored a goal. There had been a mix up in the backfield, so the other team had taken advantage of it and plowed right through their rear defensive line. Laurel's team was still up by one goal, but the girls looked spooked as if they'd lost their nerve.

Nick shot quick glances at the man and then looked away again, fairly certain he didn't catch his attention. The man had taken more than a dozen photos of the team, and it looked like he was photographing both sides. But Nick knew that was probably only a cover.

The referee blew the whistle three times, signaling that the game was over. Laurel's team had won four goals to three.

Still clutching Sophia's little hand in his, he walked back to his Hummer. When he unlocked the door, Mark slipped in the passenger side second seat quickly, after Laurel. Sophia was up in the front seat with Nick.

"So you saw the guy?" Mark asked.

"We did. Brady and Wyatt are going to follow him. My nerves are shot, Mark."

"Well, the only thing I know to take care of that then is to go get some ice cream," he announced.

Both the girls cheered.

Nick hoped they'd get some answers pretty soon. Riley was sending his guy later on that evening, and between the tracking device and questioning the man with a camera, he'd hopefully have enough certainty to be able to take his complaints to the FBI.

CHAPTER 15

"I T'S A NICE slick little piece, Nick," Kevin said.

Nick had been surprised that Riley sent his chef, but it turned out Kevin had also been trained in listening devices and counterintelligence gear when he deployed on the Zumwalt.

"And here I thought your real talent was in barbecue, Kevin. You're amazing."

Mark had a question. "So is this a U.S. manufacturer or something you buy overseas? Any idea where you would pick up one of these?"

"These are probably stolen from one of our agencies perhaps. I mean, we try to keep track of everything, but I'm guessing it's our stuff, just not our guys manning it. These look like little Israeli devices we ran into one time out of the Philippines. They were using some of these tracking devices but also were capable of recording voices. Really slick tiny pieces, the state-of-the-art stuff. But this one's slightly different. It doesn't have any capability of recording voices. But it does track location. I'm going to suggest, if you don't mind, that you disable it or, rather, let me disable it. I'm going to do it outside if you agree, because some of these carry a small explosive charge with them."

Nick was sick to his stomach. "So this thing she wore on her wrist could be an explosive device? You mean he could remotely detonate it?"

"Could be. I'm going to take some pictures so we document what it looks like, and then I'm going to take it out on the patio and disable it. I'm going to immerse it in mineral oil first, and then I'm going to smash it. The oil should retard the explosion if there's going to be one."

"Let's do this like yesterday please," said Nick.

Still in the glass Pyrex container, Kevin brought the device outside. Mark followed closely behind him.

The girls were on the phone, talking to their mother and to Lilly, whose team won and got a trophy for coming in first place at the tournament. Laurel explained about her soccer game, and Sophia wanted to tell her mother and Lilly all about the ducklings, chickens, roosters, and lambs.

"Mama? Daddy said to ask you if we can have chickens. Like baby chickens. Can we please, please, please?"

Nick heard Devon saying something, and it kind of

sounded like a soft affirmative, because Sophia was jumping for joy.

"And, Mama, they have baby ducks too. They're so cute. Soft and a little scary too," she said. She tacked on her story about the duckling biting her nose. "But it didn't hurt at all. It just scared me, Mama."

Nick was going to grab the phone and add his two cents when he heard a small explosion coming from the patio. Luckily, neither Mark nor Kevin was injured, but it left a crater in the concrete slab about four inches across and two inches deep. Devon's Pyrex dish would never cook anything else ever again, and both Mark and Kevin were splattered in mineral oil.

"Holy shit, Kevin. Tell me that wasn't detonated remotely," Nick shouted.

"Nope. Packs a wallop, though, doesn't it?"

Mark was examining his shirt. "You owe me one shirt, Nick. I don't think I can get this oil out of here. But hey, thank God it didn't go off when she was wearing it. I wouldn't have thought this tiny device would make all that noise with the size of that crater."

"Well, it's mostly because everything was under pressure. That's what created the force. But I'm going to tell you, Nick, this is not the type of stuff anybody should ever put on a child's wrist. This is involuntary— well, no, it's voluntary—manslaughter if she had been injured. If he had drawn blood, he could go right back to prison for that. Your daughter could have lost her hand."

Nick remembered that the girls were still talking to Devon on the phone, and no doubt she was wondering what had happened, having heard the blast.

"I better go in and see if I can make some apologies. Thanks, Kevin. You still do some analysis on what's left here?" he asked him.

"Yeah, I'm going to save all this. I've got some evidence bags I brought. I'll seal it up and see if I can get it off to Quantico. They should be able to give me an answer definitively one way or the other within twenty-four hours. Somebody's going to know exactly what this thing was and where it came from. For me, it's just a guess."

Nick turned his back on Kevin and Mark, running inside, sliding across the kitchen floor and the living room, heading down the hallway toward Laurel's room. He grabbed the phone lying on the ground and started to let Devon know what had just occurred.

As he looked at Laurel, he told Devon, "Kevin said that if that thing had gone off when Laurel was wearing it, it could have cost her hand."

The look on Laurel's face told Nick everything he needed to know. His daughter was never going to let anybody put anything on her person again. She had learned her lesson in probably the best way possible.

But it was a close one.

Devon had not been pleased with the description of what had occurred.

"You've got to get home. You have no reason to stay in Orlando. You just hop on the first flight back. Please."

"I was going to ask you for an extra day here, but under the circumstances, I think that's wise to come home. So let me see what I can do for flights, and I'll text you my ETA."

"Love you, Dev. Be safe, and get back here where I can make sure somebody's watching over you."

"I'm working on it."

Brady called with a message they located the photographer's home, and it appears he was getting ready to leave the house, so he wanted some instructions.

"Nick, if we let him leave, then we can kind of go through his things and see if we can figure out who he is. But then if one of us goes and follows him, the other is going to be stuck here without wheels. Or we could take him with us. From what you just told me about that device, maybe it would be a good idea to bring him in to the Sonoma County Sheriff. He lives down by the fairgrounds, and I don't think we'd be spotted if we got entry to his house and searched. What do you want me to do?" Brady asked.

"Why doesn't Wyatt tail him wherever he goes, you

stay there, and I'll come pick you up if you text me the address."

Mark heard that last comment and interrupted. "I'll go pick him up. Nick, you got to stay out of this stuff. Let me go get him, and nobody's going to recognize me, because I'm not from this area. You, on the other hand? Nick, you could get in trouble for this."

Nick agreed. In advance, Brady texted the address of the property by the fairgrounds, and as he was sending the message, he also advised Nick that the photographer had left in his car. Wyatt was going to follow.

Nick insisted the girls get ready for an early bed. He drew the bath water for them and laid out their nighties. The evening security shift was just beginning as several of the vineyard workers hopped in the back of the same pickup truck and took off down the gravel driveway. The two guards would be marching around the perimeter, everybody now being on extremely high alert with the find they had made this afternoon. Nick said goodbye to Mark and sent him on his way to hook up with Brady, using Devon's car. Nick's bright yellow Hummer was going to be easily identifiable, even if Nick wasn't in it.

He put the girls to bed, giving them a little ice cream they'd picked up at the store on the way home, read a short story, and then kissed them both goodnight. To Laurel, he whispered, "You did real good today, Laurel." She didn't look at him. She hadn't been catching his gaze all evening, he realized. "Are you okay?"

"What if I was wearing that and I was in the car with Sophia and Mommy or all of us in the car together? I'm so sorry, Daddy. I just wasn't thinking, was I?"

"Well, we got it taken care of. That's why all these guys are here to help me. In my former job, we could have just gone in and grabbed everybody off the street and taken them somewhere to interrogate them, but we don't do that here, do we?"

Laurel shook her head. And then her eyes began to water, so Nick leaned over, pulled her to his chest, and hugged her tight. "It's okay, baby," he whispered in her ear and then kissed her cheek. "Don't worry about a thing. Daddy's got you. And now you know, now you know what I used to do. And how dangerous it is."

She wiped the tears from her eyes and nodded her head, her lips downturned as she glumly admitted one more time that she was sorry.

He said goodnight, checked on Sophia one last time, and found her snoring, fast asleep. He wondered what she was thinking of when she heard the blast. He was going to have to spend some time explaining what the stakes were, not to scare her but so she would stay vigilant.

As he walked down the hallway, he heard the front door open. Brady and Mark stood before him, Brady holding a box filled with electrical components, cameras, disguises, and a sheaf of papers.

Mark grabbed one wrinkled page from the top and held it over his head.

"This is evidence of a wire transfer, Nick. Somebody has wired to this man's account twenty thousand dollars. I think you now have evidence of a crime. It's not just surveillance, Nick. He's got all kinds of shit in here, and he's got pictures of the girls on the wall. Taped to the wall. Your girls, Nick."

CHAPTER 16

T HE NEXT MORNING, they still hadn't heard from Wyatt, and that spooked Nick. Devon called to say they'd landed in LA, and they'd be at the Admiral's Club for an hour before continuing on with her flight to Santa Rosa.

Nick told her he'd be picking her up.

"You have any answers yet?" she asked.

"Yes and no. We haven't heard yet from Wyatt, who was following our cameraman, but Brady and Mark found a treasure trove of stuff at the guy's house, including some small explosive devices and a huge cache of guns. Devon, there were some ghost guns and parts for making more, ammo, including modified high-capacity clips, and some drugs—lots of things the FBI is going to be interested in, as well as pictures of our girls, all three of them, taped to the wall. I don't know yet who he is, but it's coming."

"Good Lord, Nick. Who are these people?" she

asked.

"Probably people Rodriguez connected with in prison, which is right where Rodriguez should be headed again."

"Almost seems like he's in the enforcement side of things, not the murder for hire or private surveillance and security," she guessed.

"My mind was going there too."

Nick heard the loudspeaker in the background at LAX airport.

"I'm glad you'll be in the lounge. Get something healthy to eat, and try to get a little rest, if you can. Does Lilly know about the wristband and the explosion?"

"Laurel and Sophia told her on the phone. This whole weekend was a fun adventure until she was told that. Nick, I'm glad she's scared."

"Yeah, Laurel was so upset with herself last night, knowing that band could have cost her perhaps more than a hand. It could have cost Sophia her life. She feels horrible about it. I'm thinking like you. Her being scared is a good thing, much as I try to keep all that from the family. In this case, being sharp and vigilant saves lives. She's gotten that message loud and clear now."

"Oh, that sweet girl. Bless her little heart. So when does all this get turned in? Have you gotten the Sonoma County Sherriff involved?"

"Waiting for Wyatt to get back first. That's coming too."

"Well, be safe, Nick."

"You too, sweetheart. Just a few more hours, and we'll all be together again."

Nick completed the breakfast duties, and Mark showered and then helped with the girls. Kevin had returned to Portland on the last flight out of Sonoma County.

They had a wedding scheduled for the next day, and Nick was already behind. He was looking forward to Devon's efficient help. He examined his list and then requested Mark run some errands for the reception.

The girls wanted to go with him, but Nick decided against it. He found himself worrying about why they hadn't heard from Wyatt.

Brady called.

"Something's wrong, Nick. He's dropped off the face of the earth."

"Did he indicate any place the cameraman was headed?"

"I didn't hear from him after we parted. It's odd and not like him at all. I'm going back to the guy's house, get another look around."

"Do you suppose they caught Wyatt following him?"

"That's exactly why I'm going over there. I need some answers."

Mark returned with Nick's list of things for the reception. Nick folded the phone against his chest, saying, "No word from Wyatt still."

Brady agreed to update everyone, and Nick wished him luck and got ready to pick up Devon, leaving the girls in the care of Mark. Halfway to the airport, he got a call from Rodriguez himself.

"I'm calling to see if you've reconsidered, Mr. Dunn."

"I could ask the same of you. What kind of a game are you playing, Mr. Rodriguez?"

"I'm not sure I understand your meaning. This is not a game. It's a negotiation. It's a chess game, Mr. Dunn."

"Just who is the man you have following my daughter?" Nick asked.

"Again, I have no idea who you are talking about. But I will say this. You have some balls, Nick Dunn. You don't give up easily. Why, when it would be so much safer to relocate your beautiful family elsewhere, would you stubbornly cling to a dream that wasn't even yours in the first place?"

This got Nick's blood boiling. "That's where you're wrong, Rodriguez. I'm not stubborn. I never give up. It means you're on the losing side of things. Why don't you take the money I'm offering you and relocate yourself and your cronies somewhere you can work your evil plans and no one will interfere with you? I'm not going to let you take my sister's dream, not after you took her life. Don't play games with me."

He knew it was a mistake to come on so strong, but he was having difficulty controlling his anger. He kept Rodriguez waiting on the phone.

He turned off the freeway, heading down Airport Boulevard and approaching the pick-up area. A line of cars was in front of him. He pulled over after checking the time. He was still early, unless Devon's plane had already landed.

His phone pinged, a repeat of a message he must have received when he'd been talking.

"Are you there yet?" Rodriguez asked.

It was a strange question. Did the man have some tracking device on Nick's Hummer? He looked at the text message from Devon.

"We're ten minutes early. Meet us in the passenger pickup area. Love you."

Nick sprang into action, quickly maneuvering around several cars, drivers honking at his rude command of the roadway. Undeterred, he'd nearly forgotten Rodriguez was still on the phone with him.

As he inserted his truck ahead of most the waiting vehicles, he watched in horror as Devon and Lilly were manhandled, being shoved into the second seat of a black Suburban. As it sped off and away from the airport, Nick was blocked by angry drivers who didn't allow him to move an inch. All he could do was wait until the traffic unsnarled and watch as his wife and daughter were spirited away from him, powerless to do anything about it.

And then came the voice of his sworn enemy.

"As I advised you before, is it worth the safety of your family just to try to live someone else's dream, Mr. Dunn? You're talking about prices. I'm talking about something worth much more than money. Think about it, and call me when you are ready."

CHAPTER 17

NICK CALLED MARK.

"Are the girls safe?" he asked.

"Of course they are. You get Devon and Lilly?"

"He's got them."

"He? As in Rodriguez? What a stupid fuck!"

Nick heard his own voice telling everyone he wanted to handle this peacefully. That all he needed to do was discover Rodriguez' motivation.

What an idiot I've been.

He heard himself lecture everyone about not using lethal force. Right here and now, stuck in his yellow bumblebee of a truck, he could hear Rodriguez laughing at him. Throwing his reasonable side back in his face. Withholding from him two of the four most important people in his life. He was left with the realization he'd underestimated Rodriguez, not the other way around. And why was he so cocky as to assume he could outbluff the man? Why did he think he was better at outmaneuvering him?

"Nick? Nick, are you there?" Mark asked.

"Yeah, I'm here. Stuck in traffic. I've just seen Devon and Lilly shoved into a black suburban, and I couldn't do anything about it."

"The fuck you can't. You got Brady, me, and a whole bunch of shooters. Let's take this motherfucker out!" Mark paused. "You think he's at the farm?"

"Where else would he be? He wants to do a prisoner exchange. Sophie's Choice in exchange for the lives of my wife and daughter."

"You can't do that. We'll take him out first, Nick. Brady and I will do it."

"I can't ask you to do that. You've got two girls, another one on the way, your wife, your career on the Teams. Brady's been through Hell and back, twice. I can't ask him to sacrifice everything for my chance at happiness. It's not going to work that way."

"Let me call Colin Riley. Let's call the Sonoma County Sheriff's Department. Let's all go over there. We'll show the sheriff the stuff we have on our cameraman."

"I've seen everything. Even with the cash transfer, there's no proof Rodriguez is behind it. Nothing in that box identifies him."

"Call Riley, Nick. There are smart options here."

Nick could feel how Mark was tugging on him,

begging him to be logical, to try to strategize a less dangerous solution.

But it was just like what Colin Riley had said. There was only one sure-fire way a permanent solution could be had.

Rodriguez had to be wiped off the face of the earth.

Nick didn't even sign off. He just tapped the red button on his phone and hung up. He hung up on his friendship with Mark. He hung up on all the measured, careful things he'd done so well in his life, the perfect life of a gentleman farmer who had found the value and love of the land and his family, who had put down his weapons and learned to live as he never had done before.

But when it came right down to it, he was still a killing machine. His life, even the life he could still have with Laurel and Sophia, wasn't worth anything if he didn't have Devon and Lilly too. He'd failed his sister. He'd failed to protect his family. If the only way he could save them was to sacrifice himself, then there wasn't any question what the right path was.

First, he would kill the man who dared to think this Navy SEAL would allow someone to take away everything he held dear.

If he was lucky, someone's round would also find him. He didn't want to live with the promise he'd break to Devon, when she told him she didn't want him to do anything that would force her to spend the rest of her life visiting him in prison.

He wouldn't make her suffer. He'd save her life and that of Lilly's.

And he'd die like a hero.

CHAPTER 18

NICK RAN UP and over the curb, careful to avoid getting even close to any passengers waiting to be picked up. He focused on his breathing, inhaling deeply, letting out slowly. Gradually, he stopped gripping the steering wheel and quit swearing at the dirty looks and even fingers he'd gotten as he tried to get out of the prison of cars and insolent drivers.

He forgave them, because they didn't understand. How could they know that everything he held dear was slowly drifting away from him. He had just a few more hours to fix what he could fix, and then the world could go fuck itself.

Corey answered his call on the first ring.

"Hey, Nick. Great game on Sunday, wasn't it? Laurel looks stronger every time she goes out."

He didn't want soccer. He didn't want to chitchat. One quick communication and then he'd be out of her hair.

"Listen, Corey. Mark is alone with Sophia and Laurel. What I thought was going to be a quick trip to pick up Devon and Lilly has turned complicated, and—"

"Oh gosh. Did they miss their flight? Travel by air is so bad these days."

"Something like that, Corey. I have some place I have to be. I can't get hold of Mark, and I want to make sure he's okay with the babysitting."

"Of course. I'll drop by. What do I do if he's out with the girls? Or there's nobody home?"

"Just text me. I'll figure something out."

"You want me to take the girls?"

That hurt. So much for keeping her distance. "Thought you didn't want to get involved?"

"I'm rethinking that. Wasn't very fair of me to spring that on you with everything else that's going on."

She was inching closer and closer to asking him, and he didn't have that much time. Way down the freeway, he saw the black Suburban turn onto Highway 12. One way was due west, leading to the coast. The other way, east, led to Bennett Valley Road and his farm, along with the Rodriguez ranch next door. He was going to guess that's where they were headed, but it would be a good idea if he could speed up and know for sure.

"So did anything come of the guy taking the pictures?"

"Not sure yet. I haven't heard from Wyatt."

"Today in the paper, there was an article about how Rodriguez is suing the County of Sonoma, the DA's office, and a bunch of other people."

"Yeah. Knew about that. I'm one of them. I've been told not to worry. Anyway, I'm more concerned that the girls and my friend Mark doesn't feel like I'm abandoning them. I would have brought them if I'd known about this change of plans."

"Well, I'm happy to help. It will be good to hear all about their trip. Tell Devon we're happy to have her back."

"Yes, I will be too."

He caught a slight glimpse of the distinctive taillights of the Suburban as it traveled on the connector road to Bennett Valley, with the sky turning a beautiful turquoise, highlighted with an orange glow along the western horizon. The colors reminded him of a Maxwell Parrish painting.

It would be dark soon. He had everything he needed bolted to the underside of his seat, easy to get to and unlock. He was going to don his black clothes, go into complete radio silence, and wear the greenish-black face paint he hadn't worn in years. He had his night vision scopes, his Kevlar vest, and plenty of rounds— more than enough to get the job done.

There was an electric utility access road behind the most north-facing boundary of his property, between his land and that of Mr. Rodriguez. He didn't bring his keys, so he would have to use the bolt cutters to get access to the metal shed they used to house the new tractor. The pitch of the roof was perfect and wouldn't put a strain on his back. If he was lucky, he'd be able to look right into Rodriguez's house. If not, he'd have to find a tree or perhaps climb one of his outbuildings.

Once the gate was open, the sky had turned completely black. Nick fiddled with the lock until he could wrap the curved beak of the cutters around it, and it fell to the ground, severed. He drove through then went back and closed the gate as if it was still locked. Careful to move slowly and not cause attention to himself, he parked the Hummer on the backside of the shed, out of view from the house and also the wedding center.

He swung his black duffel bag over his shoulder after checking the contents to make sure everything was there, propped a ladder against the north wall of the shed, and climbed up onto the metal roof comfortably. Flattening himself out on his belly, he assumed the position for a nice, clear shot.

He didn't have to wait long before he first heard and then saw Devon objecting and arguing with one of Rodriguez's men. The guy was about to slap her when

Rodriguez entered the room and said something in Spanish. He was carrying two glasses of what appeared to be water. Rodriguez handed one to Devon and the other to Lilly, both tied with zip ties to a wooden armed chair. They had to round their backs and slurp from the cups precariously held in one hand.

He changed his clothes, applied the face paint, and strapped on his Kevlar vest.

Using his NV scopes, he noticed Devon had continued to mouth off, now at Rodriguez. Lilly looked petrified.

His enemy sat across from them in a comfortable easy chair, put the cell phone up to his ear, and waited for an answer.

Nick saw his screen flash, but he'd put it on silent mode. After a few tries, Rodriguez gave up.

He phoned several other numbers and had discussions.

If the angle had been better, he would have drilled a nice hole in his forehead. But he couldn't do it and risk hitting either of his two girls, so he waited for another opportunity.

His phone flashed again, and this time it was Corey. He let it go to voicemail. Whatever she had to say was going to have to wait. He got a text a minute later, *Have taken the girls to my place. Mark said he was out with Brady, trying to locate you. Is everything okay?*

Again, he ignored the message and put his goggles

back on, looking for his opportunity.

His long gun still had the silencer he used in Afghanistan. He'd kept the equipment cleaned on a yearly basis and always wiped them down, storing them in the nylon and foam bag specially made for the weapon and extra equipment, where it assumed its place under the front seat of the Hummer.

He heard a barking dog and found a security guard was patrolling the perimeter with a black Doberman. He examined them both with the scopes, made the decision not to sacrifice the animal, but considered getting rid of the guard.

But then the element of surprise would be lost, so he went back to watching his wife and daughter, ready to blow off any hand attempting to touch either one of them.

He caught a break when Rodriguez appeared at the back door and then walked out onto his cracked and near-destroyed patio to have a smoke. He aimed for the upper left side of his chest and squeezed the trigger.

He wasn't used to the kick since it had been several years since he'd hunted or target practiced with this particular weapon, but he was sure his shot, unsighted and horribly inaccurate, went wide. Way wide.

And yet, Rodriguez fell. So did the security guard. Neither one of them moved as the Dobie whined and licked the guard's face, then barked at Rodriguez as if he blamed him for the shot. The dog apparently was untouched.

"What the hell?" he whispered, repositioned his scopes on top of his head and scanned the area. Two others on Rodriguez' team came running, one of them capturing the dog. Nick thought he was seeing things when he watched the men untie Devon and Lilly, order them at gunpoint to walk toward a parked van after instructing them to hoist their bags over their shoulders.

They had nearly reached the van when Nick noticed Devon had unzipped Lilly's bag and they both moved their hands inside it. The two ladies briefly looked at each other. Then Devon nodded, and in a flash, both whirled around, Lilly dropping the bag with a thud as they swung their bats at the heads of the two remaining guards. Devon aimed her second shot at the groin area. Lilly took another whack at the other guard's head, just like Nick had taught her with the pumpkins.

He slowly stood, dumbfounded with the events played out in front of him. And, even though it was pitch black, suddenly the sun seemed to shine on his head, his shoulders. He could hear the waves crashing on the sand. He was transported to some beautiful place where they all could live in idyllic bliss forever.

"I must be going insane," he whispered.

He didn't care if it was real or it was an illusion; he'd take that illusion any day.

CHAPTER 19

THE WHOLE VALLEY floor lit up like a wildfire. Flashing lights were everywhere. Sirens blared. Even two huge fire trucks traveled the short distance from the Bennett Valley Fire Station to the Rodriguez property.

Brady arrived in his truck from one corner of the property. Mark arrived from another driving Devon's car. Zak walked onto the patio on foot. The trio was cool, not making eye contact, attending to the girls and helping wrap them in blankets, calling people with their cells, and offering to take the ladies home.

But that's when Nick arrived in his Hummer. Devon ran to him, but Lilly got there first.

He knew they were talking to him, but Nick was studying the three amigos, the men who achieved what Nick had been contemplating.

But no one said a word about it.

IT WASN'T UNTIL several months later Nick could even talk with Devon about how they had landed near fatal skull fractures, in self-defense, on the two guards. Lilly wasn't laughing or telling her friends about the training her father had given her. Afterall, it wasn't party time.

They did what had to be done.

He often wondered what the sheriff did when he found all the evidence of multiple shooters. One thing he didn't do? He didn't charge anyone with the action, because he said it was obvious the guards had killed their boss and the others for their own purposes, and then the girls whacked the hell out of the guards.

RODRIGUEZ'S FAMILY WAS more than happy to accept a sum of just under four million for the old farm. Nick paid them the six million he had been willing to pay. The investors were happy, and the family was going to be able to get a fresh start somewhere else. He was told they moved back to Mexico where they could live like kings.

And Lilly and Laurel and Sophia? What did they want?

Nick and Devon together built a huge chicken complex and incubation station. They built a pen for the baby goats Laurel wanted so badly. Sophia got her ducks, and Lilly got her pitching coach.

Nick and Devon took a long vacation, filled with

sunsets and white sand beaches, wore little clothes, and never checked their cell phones one time during the two weeks they were gone.

She began baking those world-class tarts and pies again.

And Nick became the gentleman farmer, just like he'd always dreamed he could.

And they found their *real* Happily Ever After.

Did you enjoy Deal with the Devil? Watch for the next new book in the Sunset SEALs series, Finding Home.

If you'd like to read Sharon's original SEAL Brotherhood Series, you can find all the books here, or read the Ultimate SEAL Collection Vol 1, which contains the stories of the first four books in the series, along with two prequel novellas. Nick and Devon's story is in that bundle too, the story of how they fell in love, ten years ago.

authorsharonhamilton.com/seal-brotherhood

ABOUT THE AUTHOR

 NYT and USA/Today Bestselling Author Sharon Hamilton's SEAL Brotherhood series have earned her author rankings of #1 in Romantic Suspense, Military Romance and Contemporary Romance. Her other *Brotherhood* stand-alone series are: Bad Boys of SEAL Team 3, Band of Bachelors, True Blue SEALs, Nashville SEALs, Bone Frog Brotherhood, Sunset SEALs, Bone Frog Bachelor Series and SEAL Brotherhood Legacy Series. She is a contributing author to the very popular Shadow SEALs multi-author series.

Her SEALs and former SEALs have invested in two wineries, a lavender farm and a brewery in Sonoma County, which have become part of the new stories. They also have expanded to include Veteran-benefit projects on the Florida Gulf Coast, as well as projects in Africa and the Maldives. One of the SEAL wives has even launched her own women's fiction series. But old characters, as well as children of these SEAL heroes keep returning to all the newer books.

Sharon also writes sexy paranormals in two series: Golden Vampires of Tuscany and The Guardians.

A lifelong organic vegetable and flower gardener, Sharon and her husband lived for fifty years in the Wine Country of Northern California, where many of her stories take place. Recently, they have moved to the beautiful Gulf Coast of Florida, with stories of shipwrecks, the white sugar-sand beaches of Sunset, Treasure Island and Indian Rocks Beaches.

She loves hearing from fans through her website: authorsharonhamilton.com

Find out more about Sharon, her upcoming releases, appearances and news when you sign up for Sharon's newsletter.

Facebook:
facebook.com/SharonHamiltonAuthor

Twitter:
twitter.com/sharonlhamilton

Pinterest:
pinterest.com/AuthorSharonH

Amazon:
amazon.com/Sharon-Hamilton/e/B004FQQMAC

BookBub:
bookbub.com/authors/sharon-hamilton

Youtube:
youtube.com/channel/UCDInkxXFpXp_4Vnq08ZxMBQ

Soundcloud:
soundcloud.com/sharon-hamilton-1

Sharon Hamilton's Rockin' Romance Readers:
facebook.com/groups/sealteamromance

Sharon Hamilton's Goodreads Group:
goodreads.com/group/show/199125-sharon-hamilton-readers-group

Visit Sharon's Online Store:
sharon-hamilton-author.myshopify.com

Join Sharon's Review Teams:

eBook Reviews:
sharonhamiltonassistant@gmail.com

Audio Reviews:
sharonhamiltonassistant@gmail.com

Life is one fool thing after another.
Love is two fool things after each other.

REVIEWS

"Well to say the least I was thoroughly surprise. I have read many Vampire books, from Ann Rice to Kym Grosso and few other Authors, so yes I do like Vampires, not the super scary ones from the old days, but the new ones are far more interesting far more human than one can remember. I found Honeymoon Bite a totally engrossing book, I was not able to put it down, page after page I found delight, love, understanding, well that is until the bad bad Vamp started being really bad. But seeing someone love another person so much that they would do anything to protect them, well that had me going, then well there was more and for a while I thought it was the end of a beautiful love story that spanned not only time but, spanned Italy and California. Won't divulge how it ended, but I did shed a few tears after screaming but Sharon Hamilton did not let me down, she took me on amazing trip that I loved, look forward to reading another Vampire book of hers."

"An excellent paranormal romance that was exciting, romantic, entertaining and very satisfying to read. It had me anticipating what would happen next many times over, so much so I could not put it down and even finished it up in a day. The vampires in this book were different from your average vampire, but I enjoy different variations and changes to the same old stuff. It made for a more unpredictable read and more adventurous to explore! Vampire lovers, any paranormal readers and even those who love the romance genre will enjoy Honeymoon Bite."

"This is the first non-Seal book of this author's I have read and I loved it. There is a cast-like hierarchy in this vampire community with humans at the very bottom and Golden vampires at the top. Lionel is a dark vampire who are servants of the Goldens. Phoebe is a Golden who has not decided if she will remain human or accept the turning to become a vampire. Either way she and Lionel can never be together since it is forbidden.

I enjoyed this story and I am looking forward to the next installment."

"A hauntingly romantic read. Old love lost and new love found. Family, heart, intrigue and vampires. Grabbed my attention and couldn't put down. Would definitely recommend."

PRAISE FOR THE
SEAL BROTHERHOOD SERIES

"Fans of Navy SEAL romance, I found a new author to feed your addiction. Finely written and loaded delicious with moments, Sharon Hamilton's storytelling satisfies like a thick bar of chocolate." —Marliss Melton, bestselling author of the *Team Twelve* Navy SEALs series

"Sharon Hamilton does an EXCELLENT job of fitting all the characters into a brotherhood of SEALS that may not be real but sure makes you feel that you have entered the circle and security of their world. The stories intertwine with each book before...and each book after and THAT is what makes Sharon Hamilton's SEAL Brotherhood Series so very interesting. You won't want to put down ANY of her books and they will keep you reading into the night when you should be sleeping. Start with this book...and you will not want to stop until you've read the whole series and then...you will be waiting for Sharon to write the next one." (5 Star Review)

"Kyle and Christy explode all over the pages in this first book, *[Accidental SEAL]*, in a whole new series of SEALs. If the twist and turns don't get your heart jumping, then maybe the suspense will. This is a must read for those that are looking for love and adventure with a little sloppy love thrown in for good measure." (5 Star Review)

PRAISE FOR THE
BAD BOYS OF SEAL TEAM 3 SERIES

"I love reading this series! Once you start these books, you can hardly put them down. The mix of romance and suspense keeps you turning the pages one right after another! Can't wait until the next book!" (5 Star Review)

"I love all of Sharon's Seal books, but *[SEAL's Code]* may just be her best to date. Danny and Luci's journey is filled with a wonderful insight into the Native American life. It is a love story that will fill you with warmth and contentment. You will enjoy Danny's journey to become a SEAL and his reasons for it. Good job Sharon!" (5 Star Review)

PRAISE FOR THE
BAND OF BACHELORS SERIES

"*[Lucas]* was the first book in the Band of Bachelors series and it was a phenomenal start. I loved how we got to see the other SEALs we all love and we got a look at Lucas and Marcy. They had an instant attraction, and their love was very intense. This book had it all, suspense, steamy romance, humor, everything you want in a riveting, outstanding read. I can't wait to read the next book in this series." (5 Star Review)

PRAISE FOR THE
TRUE BLUE SEALS SERIES

"Keep the tissues box nearby as you read *True Blue SEALs: Zak* by Sharon Hamilton. I imagine more than I wish to that the circumstances surrounding Zak and Amy are all too real for returning military personnel and their families. Ms. Hamilton has put us right in the middle of struggles and successes that these two high school sweethearts endure. I have read several of Sharon Hamilton's military romances but will say this is the most emotionally intense of the ones that I have read. This is a well-written, realistic story with authentic characters that will have you rooting for them and proud of those who serve to keep us safe. This is an author who writes amazing stories that you love and cry with the characters. Fans of Jessica Scott and Marliss Melton will want to add Sharon Hamilton to their list of realistic military romance writers." (5 Star Review)

"Dear FATHER IN HEAVEN,

If I may respectfully say so sometimes you are a strange God. Though you love all mankind,

It seems you have special predilections too.

You seem to love those men who can stand up alone who face impossible odds, Who challenge every bully and every tyrant ~

Those men who know the heat and loneliness of Calvary. Possibly you cherish men of this stamp because you recognize the mark of your only son in them.

Since this unique group of men known as the SEALs know Calvary and suffering, teach them now the mystery of the resurrection ~ that they are indestructible, that they will live forever because of their deep faith in you.

And when they do come to heaven, may I respectfully warn you, Dear Father, they also know how to celebrate. So please be ready for them when they insert under your pearly gates.

Bless them, their devoted Families and their Country on this glorious occasion.

We ask this through the merits of your Son, Christ Jesus the Lord, Amen."

By Reverend E.J. McMalhon S.J. LCDR, CHC, USN
Awards Ceremony SEAL Team One
1975 At NAB, Coronado

Made in the USA
Coppell, TX
17 August 2022

81645520R00125